"Sooner or later, I'm going to discover what you're hiding."

Alex stood in front of her, his stance imposing as he continued. "Why don't you save us both some time and enlighten me?"

Chelsea's lips thinned. She was so distressed she barely seemed to notice when Alex reached for her hands and started rubbing them gently, his eyes locked with hers. When he spoke, his voice was softer but still insistent. "I don't know what you're involved in, but somebody tried to kill you today, and I just pulled you out of a building with a dead body in it. It's time to end the secrets. Whatever this is has gone way too far."

Chelsea's heart was thumping against her chest. She realized that her breath was coming in gasps, so she tried to slow things down and steady her nerves. What was she supposed to do?

The thought came to her then. *Trust him...*

But could she?

Books by Kathleen Tailer

Love Inspired Suspense

Under the Marshal's Protection
The Reluctant Witness
Perilous Refuge

KATHLEEN TAILER

is an attorney who works for the Supreme Court of Florida in the Office of the State Courts Administrator, where she works on programs that are designed to enhance and improve dependency courts throughout the state. She previously worked for the Florida Department of Children and Families, handling child-abuse cases both as a line attorney and in the DCF General Counsel's Office. She enjoys teaching business law online classes at Liberty University and working on finding homes for orphans with the Open Door Adoption Agency. She and her husband have eight children, five of whom they adopted. When not in the office, Kathleen spends most of her time cheering for her kids at different events or spending quiet time (hah!) at home. Kathleen has previously published three articles for *Fostering Families Today,* a magazine for foster families. She also plays drums on the worship team at Calvary Chapel Thomasville.

PERILOUS REFUGE

KATHLEEN TAILER

HARLEQUIN® LOVE INSPIRED® SUSPENSE

Recycling programs
for this product may
not exist in your area.

™ LOVE INSPIRED BOOKS

ISBN-13: 978-0-373-44635-3

Perilous Refuge

www.Harlequin.com

Printed in U.S.A.

Be strong and courageous. Do not be terrified;
do not be discouraged, for the Lord your God
will be with you wherever you go.

—*Joshua* 1:9

Family comes in many forms.
This book is for my magnificent family:
my husband, Jim, and all eight of my children—
Bethany, Keandra, Jessica, Nathan, Joshua, Anna,
Megan and James. It is also for my incredible
church family at Calvary Chapel in Thomasville,
Georgia. Thank you all for your love and support!

PROLOGUE

Cecilia Rigo rubbed her forehead, but the ache simply wouldn't go away. It was past two in the morning, but Mr. Roderick Carver, CEO of Carver Enterprises, wanted to go over the books one more time, and she would do as her employer asked. They could go over them fifty more times, but the numbers wouldn't change and neither would the fact that someone had been skimming large sums of money from the real-estate company. Cecilia closed her eyes and leaned back in her chair. Everything pointed toward Justin Carver, her boss's only child, as the guilty party, but Mr. Carver was desperately searching for any other answer.

Cecilia looked over at Mr. Carver and noticed the grayness of his skin and the heavy lines around his eyes. He seemed to have aged thirty years as the knowledge of his son's treachery seeped within him.

"I think I'll go get us some coffee," she said softly. She met his eyes and gave him a tired smile, then patted his hand and left for the kitchen. She had worked so long and closely with him that he had become a father figure to her, and she wanted to do whatever she could to ease the pain he was undoubtedly feeling.

"Thank you, Cecilia. I don't know what I would do without you." His voice was rough, and she knew he was holding back the tears.

She went to the kitchen and prepared the coffee, then pulled two cups from the cabinet. The gunshot shocked her so much that she dropped one of the mugs and it shattered against the tiled floor. She rushed back to the room to see Justin standing over his father's inert body, the blood from the older man's head wound already seeping silently across the desk.

Justin smiled at her, but it was a sinister smile and fear swept down her spine. "Just in time, my dear. I'm afraid my father shot you and then killed himself when he found out how you had been stealing from him." He pointed the gun at her chest. "Not even those pretty brown eyes of yours could convince him to spare your life. It's sad, really. What a waste." He narrowed his eyes. "Now move slowly into the room."

Despite the fear that was coursing through her body, she somehow managed to form a vehement reply. "I never stole from him. You're the one that has been embezzling money and padding your own personal accounts."

Justin shrugged. "That may well be true, but I can always forge some documents to shift the blame to you if necessary. It's a pity that you won't be here to defend yourself."

Cecilia didn't think. She threw the remaining mug at Justin's head and hit the ground, just as another gunshot rang out and the bullet hit the chair cushion beside her. A puff of feathers flew into the air as she quickly crawled on her hands and knees back toward the kitchen, her heart banging against her chest. Another bullet hit the drywall just above her head as she reached the kitchen, got to her feet and started running down the hallway. The next bullet grazed her cheek and she could feel the blood, wet and sticky, dripping down her neck. She barely noticed the pain as she darted into the library.

"There's no place for you to go," Justin called out loudly, his voice matter-of-fact. "My people are all over this building and the grounds, as well." His footsteps echoed off of the tiled floor as he followed her down the hall, and with each step Cecilia shook even more. He was so confident in his words that he walked in an even gait with no hurry whatsoever. She tried to slow her breathing so the sound wouldn't give her location away, but she was so scared she could barely control her gasps for air.

She looked desperately around the room but didn't see any place to hide from her pursuer. Her adrenaline surged as she heard the footsteps coming closer and closer. To the left she caught sight of the exit to the balcony and she flung herself through the double doors and looked urgently around the gardens below. They were on the third story of the building and she had never been good with heights. A wave of vertigo swept over her, but she had no other options.

With a quick prayer, she quickly closed the doors behind her, then put her leg across the railing and hoisted herself over, searching for toeholds in the redbrick that would keep her from tumbling to the ground. Slowly she maneuvered her body onto a small ledge underneath the balcony and into the shadows. Her right foot slipped and she let out a soft cry, but the sound was masked by Justin throwing open the door and stepping out onto the balcony himself. Thankfully, she was able to wedge herself against the ornate marble window dressing and hold herself immobile.

She could hear Justin saunter confidently to the railing, and she tried to hold her breath as his shoes clicked on the balcony tile. With each step, she grew more certain that he would discover her hiding place and her life would be over. Her heart was beating so frantically that it was ringing in her ears and a wave of nausea caught in her throat.

Suddenly, Justin's cell phone buzzed and broke the silence. Her body jolted with surprise and she nearly lost her hold.

"No, she's not here," Justin said loudly, his voice tinged with frustration. "Looks like she jumped, but I don't see her anywhere below, so she must have made it." He hit his hand against the railing. "I can't believe this! You had better find her! She can't be allowed off the property. Do you hear me? I want her dead!"

ONE

One month later

"She's a fortune hunter, Miss Abigail. She's going to rob you blind and you won't even know it until she's three states away, sipping margaritas on the beach somewhere in a designer bathing suit she bought with your money." Alex ran his hand through his hair in frustration. Apparently nothing he said would convince his client that she had made a mistake and hired a con artist as an accountant.

He glanced over at Chelsea Rogers who was making a purchase at the nearby airport newsstand, glad that she was far enough away that she couldn't hear the conversation. As she paged through a magazine, he saw her absently rub at her cheek, thumbing over a spot he knew held a small scar—the sort of one would get from a bullet graze. What kind of woman had a scar like that? And what trouble would her past bring to one of his law practice's most vulnerable clients?

"Pah, I don't believe a word of it. Chelsea is a sweetheart," Miss Abigail replied in a matter-of-fact tone.

Alex grimaced. "I'm not sure just how she cajoled

her way into your heart so quickly, but I'm not going to let her get away with it." He knew firsthand the trouble conniving women could cause—he'd been victim to one himself. And Miss Abigail had much more to lose.

"You worry too much," Miss Abigail said gently as she gave him a reassuring smile. "But I'm glad you're coming along on this trip."

Alex rolled his eyes. As soon as he had found out about Chelsea Rogers, he had a booked a ticket to accompany the two to Hawaii. Apparently nothing he said at this point was going to change Miss Abigail's mind, so the only other thing he could do was keep an eye on Chelsea *personally* and prove her dishonesty before Miss Abigail executed the new will and trust that she had demanded. Miss Abigail came from old money, and her estate was worth several million dollars. Alex, and his father before him, had been her attorney for the past thirty-two years, and Alex was not about to let her go through with her plans to leave Chelsea Rogers—a woman Miss Abigail hadn't even known a month before—as executor of the estate.

He glanced at Chelsea once again out of the corner of his eye. She was still at the newsstand standing by the cash register. He had only met her in person this morning, at the airport. So far she had been extremely accommodating and helpful, but wasn't that the way of fortune hunters? Didn't they do anything and everything to ingratiate themselves into the good graces of their benefactors? The lady had been constantly at Miss Abigail's side as they had traipsed through the airport, being helpful in courteous ways that only irritated Alex more.

He ran his hands through his hair, then tried again,

keeping his voice low so that only Miss Abigail could hear him. "Miss Abigail, what did Chelsea say to you to convince you that you need to provide for her?"

Miss Abigail looked at him as if horns had sprouted out of his head. "What are you talking about?"

"I'm just trying to figure out what Chelsea did or said to suggest that she should be in charge of your estate, should anything happen to you."

"She didn't say a word. I have been in this world eighty-three years, Alex Sullivan. I think I've had a chance to hone my skills at judging a person's character. Chelsea is a sweet girl with a good head on her shoulders. She'll make sure everything is handled correctly, and the salary I've factored in for her to receive while she handles it will make sure she has plenty of time to find a new job afterward."

Alex set his lips in a thin line. "It's simply not in your best interest to trust so much to someone you don't know very well. What of her background? Her family? You know next to nothing about this woman…"

The older lady sniffed, then turned and peered at him intently. "Tell me the truth. I know you've been investigating the girl. Have you discovered anything in her background that makes you suspicious?"

"I can barely find *anything* about her, which is suspicious enough on its own. I have the feeling she's using a false name."

He expected Miss Abigail to have a strong reaction to that, but she just looked thoughtful and nodded. "Yes," she said. "I suppose that would make sense."

Alex was flabbergasted. "Why aren't you surprised or upset that she's been lying to you?"

"Because she hasn't been—not about anything important. I realize that Chelsea has secrets. She has been frightened and jumpy since she arrived. She's wary of being out in public, and she seems to be somewhat scared of men. She shared with me that she's trying to keep a violent man with lots of resources from finding her—an ex-boyfriend, I assume. There's an awful lot of domestic violence in this world, but just because she has been victimized in the past doesn't mean she doesn't deserve my trust."

Alex frowned, clearly surprised. This wasn't the explanation he'd been expecting…but he had to admit, it made sense. It even fit with the unusual scar on her cheekbone. He had absolutely no tolerance for men who abused women—if Chelsea Rogers had escaped from that sort of situation, then he had to admire her for it. But even if it was true, that still didn't mean it was the whole story.

"If she's so wary of being out in public and talking to people for fear of being found by her ex, how did she end up working for *you?*" he asked.

"She responded to an ad I placed in a health magazine," Miss Abigail replied. Her aged fingers smoothed and re-smoothed the fabric of her dress. "I've told very few people this, not even your father when he was my attorney, but I have a rare blood type called Bombay blood. When I say rare, I mean really rare, but of all of the people on this planet, Chelsea actually has the Bombay blood type, as well. I can't have regular transfusions during surgery, because if I get any other type of blood besides Bombay blood, it would be fatal for me. I've been banking blood in advance for this Crohn's surgery I'm having in Hawaii, and Chelsea has also been donating. About a month ago she showed up on my doorstep and explained that she had seen my ad and that she had the same Bombay blood. We had her tested and found out that her blood would work perfectly." The elder lady paused, then looked Alex directly in the eye. "She didn't ask for a job, mind you. That was my idea. Of course I was already planning to pay her for her time and effort for her donations, but once I met her, I thought she would be the perfect traveling companion. She couldn't be any sweeter, and no matter what happened in her past, I have witnessed her caring and compassion firsthand. Those personality traits are a rare combination these days."

She reached over and patted Alex on the hand. "So you see? There's nothing to worry about. Now start relaxing and enjoying this trip to Hawaii."

Alex gave her a smile, noticing the tired lines on the matron's face. He didn't agree with her decision, but he didn't want to badger her any further. "Okay, Miss Abigail. You win for now, but I'm going to continue my investigation."

He watched her settle back with her puzzle book, then pulled out his laptop. He emailed the private investigator he'd hired this new information about Chelsea Rogers's rare blood type and a "violent man with resources," then continued researching on his own, trying to find out anything he could about the mysterious woman.

He automatically angled the laptop to obscure the screen when he heard someone approach and take the seat next to him, but it wasn't Chelsea, just a stranger wearing a Braves baseball cap. Alex laughed to himself. The Braves didn't have a chance this year. They had traded their best pitcher and he doubted they would even make it to the playoffs.

The man was totally engrossed in devouring a sausage biscuit while he messed with his phone. He punched a few more buttons, then put the phone up to his ear.

Suddenly he sat up straight. "This is Kent." There was a pause as he wiped his mouth with a napkin. "I'm still in Atlanta, but I might have a change in plans. I think I found the…package we've been looking for. I just sent you a picture via email to verify I found the right one."

Something in the man's tone sounded odd to Alex and he sneaked a glance over to the side. The stranger— Kent—didn't seem to notice Alex's attention. His eyes were, instead, firmly focused on the newsstand…right where Chelsea was standing.

"By accident, really," the man said as he shrugged. "I was heading back to Chicago and came across it at the airport. I've been keeping my eyes open and searching for it ever since you hired me." The man took a sip of coffee and then dug into his bag, pulling out a sheet of paper, an envelope and a pen. "Unknown, but I'll be happy to find out." He scribbled something on the paper before sealing it away in the envelope. There was another pause. "Understood. You want that pleasure all to yourself. Don't worry. I'll take care of it." He snapped his phone shut and leaned back with a smile.

Suddenly the man stood, walked down the row of seats and then turned and started walking straight toward Chelsea. Alex tensed, on alert to see if the man would try to interact with her in any way. He had seemed to be watching her closely during his cryptic phone call. Was Chelsea somehow connected to the package he'd mentioned? She looked wary as the stranger approached, but there was no hint of recognition on her face. He brushed past her without a word, but when he walked away, Alex noted that the envelope that had been in his hand earlier was now gone.

Strange. Very strange. But perhaps this was another piece of the puzzle. He'd keep working until he pieced them all together and figured out just who Chelsea Rogers really was.

"Chelsea, do you have a pen I can borrow? I thought I stowed one in my tote bag, but I can't find it."

A moment passed, then another. "Chelsea?"

Cecilia startled. She still wasn't used to answering to her new name. Everyone in Tallahassee knew her as Chelsea Rogers, a name she had borrowed from one of her favorite novels. The fake ID with the new name had cost her almost everything from her savings account back in Chicago, but it had been worth the price since they hadn't stopped her at the airport security checkpoint.

"I'm sorry, Miss Abigail. Here you go." She pulled a pen from the side pocket of her computer bag and handed it to the elderly lady.

Chelsea felt the aged fingers cover her hand. "Is everything all right, dear? You seem a bit distracted."

"I'm just a little nervous about flying," Chelsea admitted. "My stomach is a little upset." That wasn't far from the truth. Between anxiety over being out in public and her fear of flying, her stomach was in knots.

"You're not sick with something contagious, are you?" Alex Sullivan snapped his paper closed, folded it, giving Chelsea an intense stare as he did so. "Miss Abigail doesn't need to get sick during her trip."

Chelsea startled at the mysterious attorney's harsh question. She had been looking forward to this Hawaiian excursion, but ever since Alex Sullivan had joined her and the elderly lady she was caring for, the excitement had quickly disappeared. Alex had done nothing but glare at her since he'd arrived at the airport this morning, and his fierce expressions were sending cold shivers down her spine. He seemed to be watching her every move, and his perusal made her nervous and jumpy.

He's an old friend of Miss Abigail's, she reminded herself. He's not connected to Justin Carver.

But she couldn't seem to stop the nervousness she felt whenever anyone looked at her for too long or asked her too many questions. She was sure Carver was still looking for her—would today be the day he found her?

Stop. One way or another, she had to stop worrying—at least long enough to do her job. She forced her mind back to Mr. Sullivan's question.

"No, it's nothing contagious. I promise."

Alex's eyes didn't waiver. "I care a great deal about Miss Abigail. Her health and safety are my priority. I would do anything I could to protect her. I hope you realize that."

"Of course," Chelsea agreed. His antagonistic words were no surprise—his behavior had been harsh toward her all morning. She had no idea why he had joined them on this trip, and wasn't sure how she was going to manage several days in his company. Even in his casual clothing, the attorney seemed to exude intimidation and authority. His eyes slanted toward her and she quickly looked away, even as she felt goose bumps rise on her arms. She wished he wouldn't watch her so carefully. As far as she knew, she had done nothing to garner his interest. In fact, she didn't want anyone paying attention to her, and she had gone to great lengths to erase her identity and live inconspicuously under the radar for the past four weeks. If there was anything she didn't need right now it was an attorney asking questions.

She watched him fish something out of his briefcase and then snap the latches closed. He wasn't bad-looking, she decided, even if his behavior was driving her crazy. He had short dark hair and smoky-gray eyes that seemed to reach right into her soul and read her thoughts. He was also tall and broad-shouldered, towering above her five-foot-five height like a giant. She wondered how he would be comfortable in the small confines of the plane once they boarded, even in the first-class seats.

She quickly glanced away before he could nail her once again with his ferocious glare and watched a plane taxi and take off into the sky. Despite Alex Sullivan's unsettling presence, he might actually turn out to be the least of her problems. Besides the anxiety of being in such a public place, Chelsea was terrified of flying, and had been ever since a plane she had been traveling in nearly three years ago had given her the roughest flight of her life. Despite her fears, however, she hadn't been able to turn down Miss Abigail's pleas to accompany her to Maui. It was a vacation of sorts for the elderly lady, though the end of the trip included a surgical procedure for Miss Abigail's Crohn's disease, which was ultimately the reason for the journey.

Chelsea pulled out her phone and checked her messages. "Dr. Winchester's office confirmed your pre-surgery appointment," she informed Miss Abigail. "It's set for the day before the surgery." Dr. Winchester had been Ms. Abigail's doctor in Tallahassee for years, but had recently moved to Maui where he was semi-retired. The elderly lady only trusted Dr. Winchester to operate, and had planned the trip with time to play tourist for a couple of days before she actually had to report to the hospital for her procedure.

"Thank you for taking care of that, dear." Miss Abigail reached over and patted her hand. "It makes the vacation part of the trip so much more pleasant to know that you have all the other details well in hand. Hiring you to be my companion and helper for this trip was the best decision I ever made." She gave the words a peculiar emphasis, seemingly aimed at Alex Sullivan. Chelsea wondered what that was about, but decided not to ask.

She looked back at her phone, scanning again for a message she wanted to see that wasn't there—a message from the business manager of Southside Renovations, one of the shell corporations Justin Carver was using for misappropriating funds.

The only way she'd feel safe again was if Justin was in prison...but she didn't trust the police to put him there, and knew they wouldn't take her word against his without some sort of proof. She'd had too many negative experiences with law enforcement and the court system in the past to believe in that fallacy. No, if she was going to see Justin Carver imprisoned for his crimes, she'd need more evidence than her own sworn statement.

Carver Enterprises was both a real-estate acquisition and development company, and made the bulk of its earnings from buying undervalued commercial properties, renovating them and then selling them at a considerable profit. Justin had been the executive vice president, in charge of managing most of the company's renovation projects. According to the documents Chelsea had uncovered, Justin had created fictitious vendors, opened bank accounts in those vendors' names and then submitted phony invoices for renovation services that had never been performed. He then laundered the money through various businesses such as Southside Renovations before depositing them into his personal accounts in the Cayman Islands. Once the embezzlement trail had been discovered, Chelsea had helped trace more than ten million dollars that had been funneled into Justin's accounts.

According to the internet though, Southside Renovations was still in operation and had a corporate office in Hawaii. The business manager had promised to meet with her in two short days and to provide her with copies of all of Southside's latest internal accounting audits.

Knowing that Justin had committed murder and was still lining his pockets with stolen money was a bitter pill to swallow, but at least her resources indicated he'd made no attempt to cover up what he'd done or to get rid of the records. If the money laundering scheme was ongoing, then there should be plenty of evidence that could be used against him—if she could just get her hands on it. It was a long shot, but hopefully the Southside business manager would give her what she needed to put Carver away once and for all.

The manager still hadn't texted her with the location of the meet, so she stowed her phone, hoping that by the time they landed in Maui she would know a time and location when he was able to sneak away and give her the documents.

The gate agent announced the boarding call for the flight that would take them from Atlanta to Maui, and the three of them stood and gathered their belongings.

Mingled anxiety and excitement churned Chelsea's stomach as they got in line to board the plane. Would Hawaii give her the keys to free herself from fear? Or was she marching even further into danger?

TWO

As the plane began its ascent, Alex glanced at Chelsea who had a death grip on the armrest. The prospect of sitting next to this woman for the rest of the trip made him decidedly uncomfortable. He gritted his teeth. Who was he kidding? This whole trip made him uncomfortable. Alex lived an ordered life and enjoyed keeping surprises to a minimum. Spontaneity was definitely not his friend.

He checked his watch as another wave of frustration swept over him. He needed to be back in the office working his normal seventy- to eighty-hour work week, not gallivanting across the United States to some tropical paradise. Because of Chelsea, case files were piling up in his office and here he was flying halfway across the world in the opposite direction.

He looked her over suspiciously. She was actually an attractive woman. Her high cheekbones and wide chocolate-colored eyes only served to irritate him more. He didn't want to find her attractive in any way, shape or form.

About thirty minutes into the flight, Chelsea gingerly touched his arm. "Excuse me. Can you let me get by?"

"Yes, give me a minute." He closed his laptop, then got up and stowed it in the overhead bin. "Where are you headed?"

Chelsea shrugged. "Nowhere. Anywhere. I just can't sit here any longer. I'm going a little stir-crazy." She headed toward the front galley of the plane and started pacing back and forth in the tiny space as the flight attendants began serving dinner to the first-class passengers.

Alex decided to follow her. Even though the woman was an enigma, she had seemed rather sick ever since the plane had taken off and he was decent enough to want to help her when she was so obviously distressed. She certainly wasn't faking as he'd originally believed. In fact he'd never seen anyone so miserable on a plane before. He approached her from behind, intending to offer to fetch her a soda or maybe some motion sickness meds from a flight attendant.

Suddenly she turned and ran right into him. He caught her firmly in his arms and held her for a moment, surprised at how comfortable she felt there. The feeling lasted only a few seconds, but the frisson of warmth made him lock eyes with Chelsea before she pulled away. They both suddenly stepped back as if they'd been burned.

"Sorry," Chelsea mumbled. "What are you doing here?"

"I came to check on you. You looked rather pale and I didn't want you fainting in the aisle."

"I'm fine. Please don't let me disturb you. I know

you have a lot of important work to do." She shivered and hugged herself nervously.

The captain's voice came over the speaker and announced their airspeed and altitude. He then asked everyone to return to their seats due to turbulence and lit the fasten seat belts sign. Chelsea's face turned even whiter as the plane rocked under their feet. She grabbed hold of a nearby seat to steady herself and took a deep breath.

Alex saw the fear etched in Chelsea's face and reached out to support her other arm, even though she flinched at his touch. He gently led her back to their seats and steadied her as the plane continued to rock. They both looked over in Miss Abigail's direction as they returned, but she was dozing and seemed oblivious to the turbulence.

Chelsea sat, quickly fastened her seat belt and wrapped herself up again in a blanket. The plane took another dip and she grabbed on to both armrests until her fingers started turning white.

Alex noticed and carefully removed her hand from the armrest they shared and took it in his own. He gave it a gentle squeeze but didn't release it. Maybe he could distract her and learn something about her at the same time. "So why are you so scared to fly? Did you have a bad experience on a plane?"

Chelsea raised an eyebrow. "I'd really rather not relive it."

Alex shrugged. "Fair enough."

The plane jolted again and Chelsea screeched and squeezed his hand so hard it hurt. He shifted, but didn't let go. He thought a moment, then tried again. "So tell me the story of your life."

She didn't respond and he gently pushed ahead. "Come on. It's a long trip. Where were you born? Where did you grow up? These aren't hard questions." He raised an eyebrow. "Are they?"

"I'm not really in the mood for small talk," she hedged.

"Would you rather I ignore you for the rest of the trip?"

"Honestly? Yes."

Alex laughed for the first time since he'd packed his bags this morning. "Well, Miss Rogers, you must have something to hide."

Chelsea flinched and Alex was instantly alerted by her reaction. This lady was obviously scared of much more than just flying in an airplane. He wanted to demand answers, but he knew instinctively that the direct approach wouldn't work. With this woman he would have to read between the lines to discover her secrets.

He waited a few minutes for her to respond to his statement. When she didn't, he tried again. "So? Why don't you just tell me why you're so scared of flying?"

Chelsea gave an exasperated sigh. "You don't give up easily, do you?"

"Now you're getting it," he answered. "You'll find I usually get what I'm after. Maybe it would be easier if you knew that about me right up front."

"And what is it that you're after, Mr. Sullivan?"

Alex leaned closer to Chelsea, keeping his voice low. "Information, pure and simple. Miss Abigail Van Buren is one of my oldest clients, not to mention a dear friend. I'm sure you understand that it's vitally important for me to know everything I can about her associates so that I can adequately guard her interests."

Chelsea pulled her hand away and shifted uncomfortably in the seat, apparently accepting his explanation. "I was born in South America. We moved to the U.S. when I was twelve."

Alex nodded. "Ah, yes. I thought I detected a hint of an accent. Which country?"

"Brazil," she answered softly. "On a flight there to visit family a couple of years ago, my plane had some difficulties and the turbulence was horrible. We nearly crashed into a very large mountain. I've hated flying ever since."

She glanced out the window as the plane took another dip. Alex saw her start to shake and took her hand again. He waited a moment for her to relax a bit before pushing forward. "So, why did your family move to the United States?"

"I've told you about me," she whispered, not meeting his eyes. "Why don't you tell me a little about yourself?"

His brows pulled together. "Unfortunately, I don't have a very exciting story to tell. I'm certainly not a world traveler like you. I'm the oldest of three boys and have lived in Tallahassee all of my life. I spend most of my time working at my law firm with one of my brothers. My father was an attorney and he passed the business down to us. Miss Abigail has been with us since the beginning, and is one of my mother's closest friends. I am fiercely devoted to protecting her interests." His tone was businesslike yet filled with a subtle threat.

Chelsea tightened the blanket around herself. "I can understand why. Miss Abigail is a wonderful person. I know I haven't known her nearly as long as you have, of course, but I also have come to care for her a great deal."

"I'm glad," he said softly, searching her eyes for any hint of deception. "How long have you been living in Tallahassee?"

Chelsea swallowed and squeezed the blanket nervously. "About a month." She paused. "Can you let me by please? The turbulence seems to have passed and I need to go to the ladies' room."

Alex saw the withdrawal in her eyes and backed down. She was obviously hiding something, but there was no need to push for all the answers right now. With a little patience and some help from the private investigator he'd hired back in Tallahassee to research her background, he would know everything he needed to know about Chelsea Rogers in a day or two.

He stood to let her pass and glanced around at the other passengers as he did so. Miss Abigail had woken up and was doing a crossword puzzle. The lady in the seat next to her was typing furiously on a laptop and gently swaying to some music she was listening to on her headphones. Everyone else around them was dozing or watching the in-flight movie with headphones of their own.

He heard a noise behind him and noticed the man from the airport—the one with the Braves baseball cap who had made that strange phone call about a package. He was getting a bag out of the overhead bin. He wasn't a first-class passenger, but must have had to store his belongings in the first-class section due to the lack of space in the rear of the plane. The man glanced at him and nodded, then returned to rummaging around in the bag. He watched the man return to the coach seats, then sat down again and waited for Chelsea to return.

Chelsea paced back and forth in the small galley of the plane, glad to have a short reprieve from the attorney's prying questions. She didn't know why he was pushing so hard to discover her past, but discussing her history could never happen again in any context. Justin Carver was a powerful man with a very long reach. If she wanted to stay alive, she had to keep her secrets at all costs.

Chelsea took a deep breath and closed her eyes. She tried to think of something pleasant that would take her mind off the flight and the gruff attorney, but instead her head filled with images of her recent past.

The past month had been the worst of her entire life. She had been happy in Chicago. She had felt needed and fulfilled between her work and her ministries at her small Christian church. She'd lost everything that fateful day Roderick Carver died.

After the murder she had barely escaped the grounds undetected. Once away from the office building, she had been too scared to even return to her apartment. Instead she had emptied her savings account and completely abandoned her life in Chicago. The newspapers had reported Carver's death as a suicide; that he had killed himself after becoming despondent over large investment losses.

Chelsea Rogers was the only one not on Justin Carver's payroll who knew the truth about the murder. It was that knowledge that would keep her from ever leading a normal life again.

Chelsea bit her bottom lip and took a deep breath.

Two days. If the business manager from Southside Renovations could actually give her the documents he had promised and they contained what she hoped, then all of this fear and running could be over within two short days.

Her ruminations made her hands start shaking and she quickly moved them out of sight as she returned to her seat. She glanced furtively at the tall attorney, thankful that he was engrossed in the document he was studying and not paying any attention to her. These days, it was hard not to be constantly looking over her shoulder, wondering who would be a threat. Mr. Sullivan didn't seem threatening exactly, but he would never win an award for Mr. Congeniality.

She reached for her purse that was stowed under the seat in front of her and began rummaging for her gum. The crisp white envelope didn't catch her attention immediately, but she raised an eyebrow when she noticed it and pulled it out of her purse. There was no writing on the outside, but it was sealed and she could tell it had a letter or some sort of paper inside. Where had this come from? She didn't recognize it at all. A sliver of fear went down her spine as she carefully tore open the envelope and removed the single sheet of paper.

I found you and now I'm never going to let you go.

Chelsea's hands started trembling as she dropped the note back into her purse as if it were on fire. Where had this note come from? When? How had it gotten into her purse? She sank against the window as the fear consumed her. Was it from the man with the Braves cap at the airport? She thought she'd noticed him watching her, but when he hadn't said anything, she'd assumed she'd just been paranoid again. Had he slipped the note in her bag when he'd brushed past her earlier? Did the note mean that Carver had found her? If so, how? She thought she had been so careful to cover her tracks, but apparently, at some stage, she had made a grievous error.

She picked up the note again and studied it carefully, hoping she would see something that would reveal its origin. "I found you…"

She wadded it up as nausea made her stomach heave.

"Are you okay?" Alex asked from beside her, startling her. "Do you need an airsick bag?"

Chelsea shook her head quickly, aware that her situation had just gotten even more precarious. She'd forgotten that the attorney watched her every move. She didn't think he had actually seen the words on the note, but he'd certainly seen her reaction and now would be even more suspicious of her. She quickly zipped up her purse with the crumpled note inside and held it close to her chest, then tried to hide her shaking hands under the blanket.

Somehow, Carver had found her. Now there was only one question remaining. How long would he let her live?

THREE

Alex put his legal pad down and paced around the hotel room as he mentally went over his to-do list. His first priority was to contact his private detective in Tallahassee to see what he had been able to find out about Chelsea. Then he needed to convince Miss Abigail to sign the original trust documents and discard the version benefitting Chelsea. After that, he'd just need to make his plane reservations to fly back to Tallahassee.

He checked his watch, surprised at how much time had already passed since he had gotten up this morning. They had been in Maui less than twenty-four hours and the jet lag had slowed him down a bit. He pulled a number out of his wallet and dialed Tony D'Angelo, his favorite private investigator. Alex had known Tony for years, and although the man was scruffy and sloppy in appearance, he was a first-rate investigator. Tony had been an investigator for the firm for over fifteen years, but he had also been the one to discover Alex's fiancée's deception two years ago. They had been good friends ever since.

Tony picked up on the second ring, his voice loud and gregarious. "Yo, this is Tony."

"Hey, Tony. Sullivan here. Any news about Miss Abigail's assistant?"

"Some, Sully, but you're not going to like it."

A cold heaviness settled in Alex's stomach. "Lay it on me."

"Well, like we suspected, Chelsea Rogers doesn't exist. I doubt it's her real name and she's obviously taken pains to create a new identity. I'm also guessing that Abigail Van Buren is paying her under the table in cash, and that's why Chelsea's history wasn't discovered sooner. Otherwise her lack of a legitimate social security number would have tipped us off. You need to talk to Miss Abigail about that, by the way. We don't want the old lady arrested for failing to pay the appropriate taxes."

"I found some new information about Chelsea while we were on the plane," Alex offered. "She said she moved to the United States from Brazil when she was twelve years old."

"Any idea how old she is now?"

"I don't know. Late twenties? Early thirties?"

"Well, once we figure out her real name we can check with immigration to see if we can verify that story against the visa and passport records."

"Any news about this violent man with lots of resources that seems to want to find her? Miss Abigail seems to think Chelsea was a victim of domestic violence."

"None yet." Tony paused. "I've started working on the Bombay blood angle you told me about, too. I can keep digging if you want me to. The question is how far do you want me to go?"

Alex shrugged to himself. Tony charged quite a fee

for his services. How much did he really want to know about Chelsea Rogers? Once he talked Miss Abigail out of the crazy idea of making Chelsea her executor, the case would be closed from his standpoint. His client's interests would have been safeguarded. But what if Chelsea continued to work for Miss Abigail and ingratiated herself even further in the elderly lady's good graces? Or what if he couldn't convince Miss Abigail to revert to her previous will and keep Chelsea out of it?

He ran his fingers through his hair. He knew he needed to look out for Miss Abigail. He couldn't just stand by and watch her get taken to the cleaners by an unscrupulous con artist. "Take two more days. While you're searching on that end, I'll try to find out what I can from this side. I'll let you know if I come up with anything new."

"Can you overnight me something with her fingerprints on it? If she's ever been printed I can find her in the system, and that might speed things up."

Alex paused a moment. "I'll see what I can do. In the meantime, I'll wait here in Hawaii until you report in, just in case you find something." He read off the number to the hotel and his room number, then disconnected. It looked as though he would be stuck in Maui for another two days unless Tony was able to discover something sooner.

Alex laughed softly to himself. There were probably very few visitors to this lush tropical paradise that considered themselves "stuck" here—but Alex had never been the type to enjoy vacations. He liked being at work, where he could feel productive and useful. He called the firm and checked in with his brother, Ryan, then called the airline and reserved a seat home. For the next two days he would do his own research on Chelsea Rogers here in Maui to see if he could discover her secrets for himself. Between his own investigation and Tony's, surely he would find out the truth.

Chelsea adjusted the sunglasses on her nose, then scanned the pool area once more for anyone who might be watching her. She hadn't seen anyone acting suspicious, but the fear the note had inspired hadn't dissipated and she was terrified that at any moment, Justin Carver or one of his minions would approach her. She glanced over at Miss Abigail who was doing a crossword puzzle under a large blue beach umbrella. The lady had been very energetic today, despite the jet lag, and they had spent the better part of the day discussing their vacation plans and making sure all of the last-minute details were covered.

Chelsea had tried to be an enthusiastic participant in the conversations, but the note had made her jumpy and she'd found it hard to concentrate. Was the note really from Justin or one of his cohorts? If so, then she should probably be running again. Justin wanted her dead, and she had no doubt he would hunt her down and try to kill her if he truly had discovered her location. But Chelsea couldn't leave Miss Abigail, not right before her surgery—not when she couldn't even be sure the note was connected to Justin. No, for now she'd stay put—but she'd stay on alert, too.

She opened her laptop and did a search for Justin Carver, trying to see if there was any mention of his current whereabouts in the media. She found nothing recent, so she moved on to check her email. Finally.

The email from the business manager from Southside was short and succinct.

TOMORROW. SOUTHSIDE WAREHOUSE. BUILDING 149, 11 P.M.

Her heart leaped as hope swelled within her. She glanced around the pool again, then returned her attention to the screen.

A man in jeans and a blue T-shirt caught her attention and she studied him carefully as a wave of anxiety swept over her. He was the only one in the pool area that wasn't in a bathing suit, but it was more than his clothing that made him appear suspicious. Twice he had looked in her direction with a cold and calculating expression, and he seemed to be following her with his eyes. He looked familiar to her, but she couldn't quite place where she had seen him before. Was he the man from the airport yesterday? The one in the Braves cap who she suspected had planted the threatening note in her purse? Her hands started shaking and she closed her laptop with a snap.

"I think it's time to go back to the room. Don't you think so, Miss Abigail? I'm starting to get a little too much sun."

"Sure, darling. I think it's about time for my favorite TV show anyway."

The man looked in her direction a third time. Chelsea quickly got up and went to Miss Abigail's side, then helped her gather her things just as the man started to approach them. With each step he took Chelsea's heart seemed to beat faster and faster and her knees turned to jelly.

"So here's where you've been hiding."

The voice from behind made her jump and she nearly dropped her computer. She put her hand on her chest and took a fortifying breath as she turned and looked up at Alex Sullivan. "You scared me," she said with an edge in her voice.

Alex raised an eyebrow and leaned closer so only she could hear him. "Really? Who did you think I was?"

Chelsea leaned back, uncomfortable. Words failed her and she found herself both unable and unwilling to explain further. She looked over her shoulder and noticed that the man in the T-shirt had passed without incident and was effectively ignoring them. Had she been wrong about him? Was he truly a threat or was the danger only a product of her overactive imagination?

"We were just heading back to our room," Miss Abigail volunteered, giving Alex her best smile and totally unaware of Chelsea's angst. "Care to escort a couple of beautiful ladies back to the suite?"

"I'd be honored," Alex replied as he held out his arm. He patted Miss Abigail's hand when she placed it on his biceps. "Do you think you might have some time later to discuss your legal documents? I wanted to go over them with you today if we could."

"Nonsense," Miss Abigail replied. "Today is not a day for paperwork. It's a day to enjoy the sun and recover from that long airplane ride."

Chelsea ignored the rest of their banter and took one last look at the man in the blue T-shirt. He had turned now and was watching them leave with a measuring eye as he sipped his soda at the bar. Slowly he reached behind him and pulled his Braves cap out of his pocket, then he put it on and smiled directly at her.

Chelsea tightened her grip on her computer, trying to mask her fear. He was following her. He was the man from the airport. No wonder he had seemed familiar. Was he working for Justin Carver? Surely if he was, he'd have made some attempt to attack her rather than just watch her. No, her secret was probably safe—for now. But who was he and what did he want? And most importantly, how could she protect herself? Indecision pulled at her and she felt a knot tighten in her stomach. Although there were people all around her, she felt quite vulnerable and alone. What should she do? Where could she go to be safe?

FOUR

The next morning Chelsea was up early, packing the trunk of the rental car for their planned morning trip to the national park at the top of Haleakala, one of the island's volcanos. Apparently it was the best place on the island to watch the sunrise and enjoy a picnic breakfast. Chelsea stowed another bag, then closed the trunk. She was anxious to be under way. The sooner they were away from the hotel, the lesser chance she had of running into the man with the baseball cap again. So far, she hadn't seen him since the pool, but she was keeping a wary eye on her surroundings just in case.

"Are you ready to go?"

Chelsea jumped at the sound of Alex's voice and turned to see him approaching. "Almost. Miss Abigail stopped at the front desk for a moment and asked me to get these bags loaded into the car. She should be here any minute."

She picked up her camera bag and took a step back. Why was he staring at her like that? His look was so intense that for a moment she wondered if he had somehow discovered who she really was. The thought made her subconsciously retreat another step, then another.

She gave herself a mental shake. Alex couldn't possibly know who she was and she refused to believe anyone who was an old friend of Miss Abigail's could have any connection to Justin Carver. She still hadn't figured out why Alex was so intent on digging into her past, but he had been nothing but kind and compassionate with Miss Abigail, and she found herself actually admiring him for that in spite of his gruff demeanor. She remained hopeful that he would be pleasant and congenial during the day's activities. She realized that the less Alex knew about her the better. But living in such anonymity was a lonely existence and having an adult conversation with someone her own age was rare these days and even tempting.

Still, the more she thought about it, the more she realized the futility of getting to know him or anyone else any better. With Carver after her, there was no way she could have an honest or lasting friendship with anyone. The thought was a difficult reality to accept.

She glanced up at Alex's face and noted that his steel-gray eyes were still studying her. She cringed inwardly. The best course of action was just to avoid him as much as possible, despite the loneliness she was feeling. She moved toward the rear door of the vehicle. Hopefully he would leave in a day or two and forget that she even existed.

"Any idea how long this jaunt is supposed to take?" Alex asked, breaking her train of thought.

"It depends upon how much time Miss Abigail wants to spend on top of the mountain." She paused. "I thought you were too busy to spend time with us today, Mr. Sullivan. Aren't you leaving soon?"

Alex narrowed his eyes. "Eager to be rid of me?"

Chelsea shrugged. "No. I'm just trying to figure out what a busy attorney like you is doing in Maui in the first place. It's obvious you don't want to be here. You've made that quite clear."

"Have I?"

Chelsea's hands stilled. "Yes. Why are you here, Mr. Sullivan?"

Their eyes locked for a moment, neither one willing to give up any information. She looked away first and opened the car door. She didn't care about winning this battle of wills. All she really had to do was keep Alex Sullivan from discovering her past. Not only would she probably lose her job with Miss Abigail if he found out, but he would also undoubtedly make her go to the police. She wasn't ready to do that without more proof. Besides, trying to stay away from the man with the cap and worrying about the note were stressful enough. She didn't need to engage in a verbal sparring event with Alex Sullivan just because he seemed suspicious of her for whatever reason.

"Alex! I'm so glad you're joining us!" Miss Abigail gushed as she approached, giving him a big kiss. "Let's hit the road, folks. I'm not getting any younger and the sun will be up before you know it."

Alex raised an eyebrow at Chelsea, then released the door and leaned over to give Miss Abigail a quick kiss on the cheek. "Your wish is my command. Shall we go?"

Chelsea got in the backseat, the anxiety pulsing through her. Whatever Alex's reason for coming to Hawaii, it seemed he wasn't planning on leaving anytime soon. And that meant she'd have to put up with his probing stares and persistent questions for at least a while longer.

An hour and a half later, Alex, Chelsea and Miss Abigail got out of their car and made their way over to the observation look-out deck. The trip up had been uneventful, with little conversation since neither Chelsea nor Miss Abigail had wanted to distract Alex as he negotiated the narrow roadway on the way up the mountain. Although it was only twenty-two miles from the base of the mountain to the overlook at the top, the trip had taken much longer than they'd expected because of the winding roads and hairpin turns.

Once at the park, Alex unfolded the portable chairs they had borrowed from the hotel and the three of them sat and faced the east, waiting for the show to begin. By the time they were situated a faint light was already beginning to brighten the sky on the horizon. For the next twenty minutes they sat in awestruck wonder as God painted the heavens with beautiful colors and lit up the valley below with reflections of the morning light. Pale pinks and purples colored the lava beds and mirrored the pastels from the sky. It was truly spectacular.

Chelsea took several photos with her 35 mm digital camera, then stood and checked on Miss Abigail. So far she hadn't seen any signs of danger on their trip, but she constantly scanned the other tourists at the park, keeping her eyes open for the man with the Braves cap just in case he'd managed to discover her location. And what if he wasn't alone? What if the man with the cap was working with others that she couldn't recognize? Suddenly her apprehension was too much to handle and she knew she had to move around before the stress consumed her.

"Would you mind if I walked around and took a few more pictures, Miss Abigail?"

"Not at all, dear," the older lady said sweetly as she patted Chelsea's hand. "You take all the time you want. I'm just going to sit here and enjoy this marvelous view."

Chelsea smiled, then stood and started walking along the ridge to capture different angles. She was an avid amateur photographer and tried to let herself get lost in composing her photographs and enjoying the beauty around her. It didn't work—she was too tense. She heard the crunch of rock and peeked back quickly. Just Alex—not a threat to her safety, just a threat to her peace of mind. A knot tightened in her stomach as she prepared for the battle. She turned and looked at him, but instead of antagonism she saw a question in his eyes.

"Are you going to take a whole roll up here?" His voice was tinged with disbelief as he put his hands in his pockets and watched her with the camera.

Chelsea shrugged, determined that he wasn't going to rattle her today, despite his constant questions and barely veiled suspicion of her. She crouched and took another shot, getting one of the sun just as it was breaking over the horizon. "Hardly anyone uses film anymore, Mr. Sullivan. This is a digital camera, so I can take hundreds of photos and just delete the ones I don't want. Sometimes I need to take a whole slew of shots to get that one special photograph." She adjusted the focus on her Canon and peered through the viewfinder. "Do you have a hobby?"

Alex grimaced. "I don't have time for hobbies. I have a law practice to run."

"You're missing out," Chelsea said quietly. She stood and their eyes locked. Despite the frustration she saw in his gray depths, an emptiness she hadn't expected reached out to her.

Miss Abigail had told her that Alex Sullivan basically lived at his office and worked seventy-hour work weeks. Maybe she could help him enjoy a small part of Maui before he returned to that single-minded existence. She took the strap off of her neck and handed him the camera. "Pictures tell a story, Mr. Sullivan, just like an attorney giving an opening statement. Take a look."

Alex paused a moment as if considering her analogy, then shrugged and took the camera. He pointed the viewfinder toward the valley and turned slowly, looking around at the different landscape that surrounded him. "It all looks the same to me." He shrugged. "Everything is a fuzzy blur."

Chelsea laughed and gently reached over to adjust a setting on the top of the camera, then guided his index finger to the button on the top right of the body. His skin was warm and to her own surprise, she enjoyed the touch. "Okay, it's on automatic focus now. Just push this button halfway down. Yes, that's it. Now it will focus for you. When you're ready to take a shot, push the button all the way down until you hear a click."

Alex played with the focus for a while, slowly pointing the lens at different views of the valley and snapping a few pictures. Then, to her amazement, he turned the camera toward her and took a few shots. She laughed and covered her face with her hands and waved him away, but he took a few more anyway, ignoring her protests. Finally he pulled the camera away from his eye.

"So you take a hundred photos of the same thing. Then what?"

She turned the camera over and showed him how to scroll through the pictures he had taken and delete the ones he didn't want. "The best ones I print and put in albums. Occasionally, I frame one and put it on my wall. I don't buy very many souvenirs when I travel. My pictures are great reminders of my trips."

"Do you travel a lot?"

The question was asked in a casual way, but Chelsea raised any eyebrow to show that she understood that he was again probing for more information about her background.

"Not as much as I'd like. I usually enjoy exploring new places and meeting new people." She grinned pointedly at him. "Usually, that is."

Alex continued to scroll through the pictures, ignoring her subtle gibe. "So where have you visited?"

Chelsea reached for the camera, but Alex moved slightly, keeping it just out of her reach, and continued to peruse her photographs. "Several different states. A few countries. This is my first trip to Hawaii. Have you been here before?"

"No, I don't have time to travel much." He paused and then slowly looked away from her camera and captured her eyes with his own. "You've got some really pretty photos on here, and also a lot of pictures of various men—all of whom look kind of rough." He showed her one of the pictures. "Is this a friend of yours?"

Chelsea felt her pulse accelerate. Why hadn't she deleted those pictures? There had been several times since she had escaped from Carver that she had worried that someone was following her, so she had taken pictures of the suspicious men to help her remember their faces, just in case. So far, each had been a false alarm, but she'd kept up her surveillance, regardless. In her book, it couldn't hurt to be too careful. But how could she explain that to Alex? She crinkled her nose and rubbed her arms, trying to come up with a reasonable explanation for the photos and warm up at the same time. The altitude was 7,000 feet above sea level and it was definitely cooler here than it was at the beaches below.

She bit her bottom lip. Struggle as she might for a plausible reason for the photos, her mind drew a blank. She chose to evade the subject and furtively hoped that he would let it drop. "I'd better go check on Miss Abigail. Hopefully the walk will warm me up—it's kind of chilly up here. Are you ready for breakfast?"

Alex slipped off his fleece jacket and handed it to her with a frown. He'd obviously noticed that she had avoided the question, but he didn't push, despite the query in his eyes. "Here. I can't have you freezing."

She took the jacket gratefully and hugged it around her. "Thanks, I appreciate it." It warmed her instantly and smelled fresh, clean and masculine. Strange how the simple gesture of him lending her his jacket made her feel not just warmer but safer, as if she could count on him to look after her.

Strange thought, indeed. She knew better than that—she could count on no one but herself.

After returning to Miss Abigail, they breakfasted on shaved honey ham, Hawaiian sweet rolls and sharp cheddar cheese. Chelsea had also found some fresh pineapple at the deli and a few other tropical fruits to round off the meal. She had even brought a jug of freshly squeezed orange juice and little paper cups emblazoned with the hotel logo.

The food was simple yet satisfying, and Alex felt himself watching Chelsea as she served the small breakfast, filled with a sense of peace he hadn't experienced in a long time. Her eyes danced as she talked and she moved with a grace he had rarely seen. Could this woman really be a criminal? She sure didn't fit the scheming stereotype he had in his mind. But then, would any con artist be easy to spot? After all, his fiancée had sure pulled the wool over his eyes before her true character had been revealed. Irene had professed her love one day and the next tried to steal his client's secrets so she could sell them to his client's adversary. Her treachery had been a bitter pill to swallow and still squeezed his heart whenever he thought about it.

He eyed Chelsea critically. Was it possible she was just a great actress, playing a part? Who was the real Chelsea? She was definitely hiding something. His investigator's inquiries had proved that. But what? And who were all of those men on her camera? His mind swept through various possibilities as they finished breakfast, but he still didn't know enough about her to really come to any conclusions. As much as he hated to change his plans yet again, he realized that learning about Chelsea and her motives was going to take much longer than he had anticipated. He would probably need to extend his trip if he was going to find out the truth. He patted his pocket where he had stashed the paper cup she had been using and hoped that Tony would be able to get the fingerprints off of it without any problems.

Several other people were milling around the observation deck and the antics of a three-year-old boy captured his attention. The child was very energetic and was throwing rocks over the railing whenever his parents weren't looking. Alex smiled and then scanned some of the other people who were also standing along the railing. Most were engrossed with the view, but then he noticed a man wearing a Braves cap who seemed to be watching Miss Abigail and Chelsea with a careful eye. Was it the same man from the plane? He tried to remember the features of the man but couldn't recall much besides the baseball cap. Surely there was more than one Braves fan in Maui.

This man was large, with dirty-blond hair catching the light in spite of his cap. He looked to be about thirty years old. At first Alex thought he was just being overly suspicious, but as Chelsea started to pack up the remains of their breakfast and take some of their belongings back to the rental car, he noticed the man's eyes continue to follow her movements. He was definitely watching her. The hair on Alex's neck prickled. He stood abruptly and started toward the stranger.

The man seemed startled at Alex's movement and for a moment their eyes locked. The menace Alex saw was palpable, but suddenly the other man turned and quickly strode away. Alex hesitated, torn between the desire to chase the man down and demand answers as to why he was watching them or to stay and make sure the women were safe.

"Is everything okay?" Chelsea asked as she came up and stood beside him.

"You tell me," he answered, keeping his voice low enough so that only she could hear him. "There was a man watching us—Braves cap, shaggy blond hair. I think he was on our flight—but he just walked away rather quickly and disappeared toward the northern observation area." He saw Chelsea's face visibly pale at his words and she took a step back. He took a step forward. "Do you know the guy?"

Chelsea shook her head. "I don't know anyone in Hawaii."

"Are you sure? I'd say he's about thirty years old. Dark eyes, heavy. Probably a drinker by the look of his face. He seemed dangerous."

Chelsea's hands started shaking at his words and she quickly thrust them into the pockets of the jacket. "Maybe we should get Miss Abigail back to the hotel now, just to be safe."

Alex nodded, keeping a wary eye on Chelsea. "You seem pretty scared for someone who claims not to know the man."

Chelsea raised her eyes and took another step back. "I don't know anyone in Hawaii," she repeated. "I'll finish packing things up so we can go." She turned abruptly and quickly started putting up the folding chairs, effectively ending their conversation. Alex paused for a moment, torn between pushing her further for more information and letting the subject drop for now. He finally moved to her side and starting packing up his own chair, but didn't ask her any more questions. Miss Abigail was close enough to overhear them and Alex didn't want to upset or worry the elderly lady. But talk they would, as soon as they returned to the hotel. It was time to get some answers, whether Chelsea wanted to give them or not.

It didn't take them long to get Miss Abigail ensconced in the car and within a few minutes they were on the road, heading back down the mountain. Alex continued his perusal of Miss Abigail's assistant as he drove, listening carefully to every word she uttered in the hope that she would give more of herself away. Although she always had a kind word for Miss Abigail, he noticed that she never said anything personal about herself or her history during any of the conversations.

Alex eased around a bend in the road, then noticed a black SUV coming up fast behind him. The road was narrow with no space to pass, but the other driver was apparently in a hurry and immediately started riding his bumper. Alex tapped the brake and glanced in his mirror, catching sight of a man's silhouette in the driver's seat. He couldn't see the man's features, but did note that he was wearing a baseball cap and dark glasses. A wave of apprehension swept over him. Was it the man with the Braves cap?

Instead of backing off when Alex slowed, the SUV came closer. Suddenly both Chelsea and Miss Abigail noticed Alex's concern and looked behind them to see what was happening.

"Why is that man so close?" Miss Abigail asked, her tone filled with worry, her eyes wide.

"He must be in an awfully big hurry," Chelsea added. She leaned closer to the window. "Is that the same man you saw at the park?"

"I think so," Alex said tightly. He kept his eye on the SUV and at the same time handed Chelsea his cell phone. "Call 9-1-1. This guy seems determined to cause us trouble today."

Suddenly the car lurched as the SUV slammed into the rear bumper. Both women screamed and Alex tightened his grip on the wheel and tried to control the car on the narrow, dangerous road. Was this maniac trying to kill them all?

FIVE

Metal crunched as the SUV rammed the back of the sedan. The trunk took the brunt of the impact and Alex could see the damaged trunk door sticking up in an awkward angle. He hit the accelerator and the tires squealed but he was only able to get a few feet away before the SUV was back battering his bumper yet again. This time the rear window cracked upon impact and a spider web of breaks spread across the safety glass.

"Hold on," Alex said forcefully as he tried to keep the car on the road. The SUV dropped a few feet behind, but quickly regained ground and rammed them yet again. This time the bumper of the SUV caught the back right corner of the sedan, and Alex felt the car trying to spin out of control. He yanked on the wheel with all of his strength and was barely able to straighten the vehicle out before the road curved, passing a hundred-foot drop on the left. He didn't even have time to process that he had just kept them from plunging to their deaths before the SUV was back threatening them again. The larger vehicle stayed close to their car as if the two automobiles were glued together. With a burst of speed, the SUV pushed the sedan, forcing the smaller car straight for an outcrop of rocks up ahead.

Miss Abigail closed her eyes and Chelsea screamed as Alex jerked the wheel to the left, barely keeping the car on the road as he pulled away from the SUV. The two right tires came up off the highway due to the force of the turn and spun in midair for a few seconds before returning to the pavement. Smoke rose from the burning rubber as the tires squealed against the asphalt and he jerked the wheel to the right, trying to straighten the car once more. They barely missed the rocks as the rear end of the vehicle fishtailed, searching for purchase on the shoulder.

Alex quickly accelerated and jerked the car forward as the SUV rammed the back right of the car, catching the back door and the entire rear panel. Metal crunched as Alex's body slammed against the car door from the impact and his head hit the frame. The SUV pushed the sedan even farther onto the shoulder, but the car's tires finally caught and screeched as Alex pulled away, once again getting free of the SUV. He could feel a trickle of blood on his temple, but he ignored it, trying to get as far away as possible from the assailant in the SUV.

Alex glanced quickly into the backseat. "Are you okay?"

Chelsea nodded, her eyes wide. "So far. The police are on their way."

He turned his attention to his other passenger. "Miss Abigail?"

"I'm okay, son. Just get us out of here."

The larger vehicle didn't immediately follow them, and Alex checked nervously over his shoulder as the distance between the two vehicles grew. He navigated around another curve and the SUV disappeared from view completely.

"Is it over?" Chelsea asked, her voice breathless.

"No," Alex answered, his breath coming hard. "He'll be back. I think that last crash just knocked the wind out of him." He could feel the adrenaline surging as he gripped the wheel and focused on the road. A small two-door car in front of them was slowly maneuvering around the next curve, but Alex didn't have time to patiently wait for him to take the turn. He said a quick prayer as he passed on the double yellow line and zoomed ahead. A few seconds later he glanced in the rearview mirror and caught sight of the SUV passing the same car and accelerating toward them once again.

He searched the road in front of him for some sort of escape but saw nothing that could offer any refuge from the other driver's homicidal onslaught. The SUV quickly bore down on them and Alex tensed involuntarily, waiting for the impact.

The car jerked as the SUV slammed into them again and Alex hit the accelerator as they reached a straight stretch. He was only able to pull ahead by a few feet before the SUV caught the rear left bumper. This time the impact was so hard that it spun the sedan in a complete circle. Tires squealed and smoke rose from the asphalt as the car came to a stop in the middle of the road and the engine died. Alex quickly turned the key to start the car again and breathed a sigh of relief when the engine caught and roared back to life. He anxiously looked out the windows and caught sight of the SUV about fifty feet behind them. It wasn't moving, but he heard the driver racing the engine as if he were a bull about to charge a matador.

Alex quickly glanced over at Miss Abigail and, seeing that she was scared but unharmed, moved his eyes to Chelsea. Her eyes were closed and her lips moving in silent prayer, but so far she also seemed uninjured. He said his own prayer of thanks and looked back at the SUV. He still couldn't make out any features of the driver, but from this angle he could see that the man was definitely alone in the vehicle. Who was he and what was the impetus of this attack? None of this made any sense.

Suddenly the SUV came roaring toward them. Alex quickly gunned the engine. The car jolted forward but was no match for the speed of the larger vehicle, which overcame it in a matter of seconds.

"Watch out!" Alex yelled, bracing for impact. He could see the grill of the SUV bearing down upon them. His heart was beating so hard that it felt like it was about to come right out of his chest. The velocity and weight of the SUV was sure to cause major damage upon impact and might just kill them all.

At the last possible moment the SUV veered and smashed into the left front corner of the car, sending it into another spin. With a crash, the sedan stopped against an outcrop of rock. The impact had forced Alex's head to knock against the car frame a second time; this time leaving him stunned and a bit light-headed.

The car engine had died again and he fought the dizziness as he turned the ignition key and pumped the gas. The engine refused to turn over and just clicked in response. His vision clouded, out of the corner of his eye Alex thought he saw the driver approaching their vehicle. He turned the ignition key again, hoping for anything that could help them escape. A loud ringing buzzed in his ears and between that and the problems with his eyes he felt helpless to do or to say much to stop the attacker from advancing.

Chelsea screamed as the man pulled open the passenger-side back door, reached in and roughly grabbed her arm.

"You're coming with me," he said in a coarse, deep voice. "You've got a date with an old friend."

"No!" Chelsea screamed, her voice frantic. Alex reached into the backseat and grabbed her other hand to help her, but a wave of nausea swept over him and his grip was weak. He could feel her struggling but the assailant was strong and he wrenched her from Alex's grasp.

Alex felt her slip through his fingers and frantically turned to his door and pulled on the handle. He looked over at Miss Abigail who seemed to have fainted. The door was firmly wedged against the rock and wouldn't budge, despite his pushing and pulling on the handle. He finally gave up, climbed into the backseat and tumbled out the door, fighting the vertigo the entire time. As he stood, another wave of dizziness overtook him, forcing him to his knees. Sounds and sights seemed distorted, but he looked up to see Chelsea still struggling in the man's arms as he pulled her across the road toward the SUV that was parked up ahead.

Alex tried to stand but wasn't able to get to his feet. He ended up leaning back on his heels instead just as sirens sounded in the distance. Finally the police were responding to Chelsea's 9-1-1 call for help. Would the threat of law enforcement's involvement stop the attacker? He said a silent prayer, quickly asking for the Lord's protection and divine intervention.

He felt totally helpless as he watched Chelsea struggle, but a wave of relief swept over him as the assailant released Chelsea and rushed to the SUV, leaving her behind. A few moments later the tires spun as the SUV peeled off and disappeared around the bend.

"Oh, Alex. Are you okay?" Chelsea was crying as she rushed to his side and put her arms around his neck. She squeezed hard, her breath coming in frantic bursts.

"I will be. I just need a few minutes to regroup." Already his vision was starting to clear, but at the same time his head was beginning to pound ferociously. He enjoyed the hug and returned it selflessly, trying to comfort her. "How about you? Did he hurt you?"

"Not in any way that matters." Slowly her breathing returned to normal but her hands continued to tremble. She suddenly released him and rushed to the front passenger-side door of their destroyed vehicle. "Miss Abigail? Are you hurt? Is anything broken?"

Miss Abigail's breath was ragged, but she managed to shake her head at Chelsea. "I survived. What was that all about anyway?"

Chelsea's closed her eyes for a moment but didn't answer. Alex noticed that her face was pale as she looked around anxiously. "Do you think he's coming back?" she asked, her voice brittle.

"I doubt it with the police being so close, but as soon as the police get here we can give them his description so they can start a manhunt." The sirens were obviously closer, which meant they were nearly upon them. "Maybe once they know what to look for, they can send out an all-points bulletin and catch him before he gets to the bottom of the mountain."

He tried to stand again and this time made it to

his feet. His ears had stopped ringing and his vision seemed mostly restored. He returned to the side of the car and leaned heavily against it, verifying with his own eyes that Miss Abigail was unhurt. The elderly lady looked stricken, but he didn't see any visible injuries.

"Did either of you get a good look at the license plate?"

"I did," Miss Abigail volunteered. "It was one of those specialty plates with a volcano on it. I only remember the letters at the beginning, though. R-T-L."

Chelsea snapped her fingers, suddenly animated. "That's right. It said R-T-L-7-4-5. Maybe that will help identify the maniac driving that SUV."

"That's excellent." Alex nodded. "I'm so glad you got a good look. I was so busy trying to keep us alive that I didn't even have time to notice."

"You did an excellent job," Miss Abigail said as she unlatched her seat belt.

"Yes, you did," Chelsea agreed as she regained more of her control. "I've never seen such amazing driving."

Alex gave a halfhearted smile. "I wish I could take the credit, but I think we're going to have to give that to God. He's the only reason we're still alive."

A few moments later their car was surrounded by Hawaiian state troopers, an ambulance and a general sense of chaos. Chelsea and Alex had both been outside the car when law enforcement approached, but once the squad cars arrived and the officers started asking questions and examining the scene, Alex noticed Chelsea withdraw and get back into the rear seat of the damaged sedan. Was she afraid of the police? She would have to give her name and her statement to the officers at some point. He wondered fleetingly if she would give them her fake name or her real one. As horrible as the events had been, maybe now at least he would learn a little more about her.

He walked over to the demolished vehicle and leaned in. "You okay?"

She nodded but slid even farther away from him.

"You want to tell me who that man was that was chasing us?"

Chelsea shook her head. "I don't know him."

"Well, he sure seemed to know you. Why else would he drag you across the road and try to kidnap you?"

She kept shaking her head. "I don't know what to tell you. I don't know him."

Alex raised an eyebrow. "Yeah, you keep saying that. But you know why he was chasing us, don't you? And who's the 'old friend' he mentioned?"

She wouldn't meet his eyes and Alex was instantly wary. "What did you do to make him chase us? Did you rip off somebody? Is that why you're going under a false name? Is that guy here to recoup the losses?" He leaned in closer and his voice was low so only she could hear. "Did you con the wrong person, Chelsea Rogers?"

Chelsea's eyes looked stricken but she refused to answer. He was about to pelt her with more questions when he felt a tap from behind and turned, his frustration threatening to consume him.

The officer in charge of the scene introduced himself and started asking questions. Alex began explaining what had happened as the two walked away from the damaged car. At the same time the EMTs arrived and started checking Miss Abigail for injuries. A few minutes later another EMT approached Chelsea but Alex saw her wave him away just as he was finishing up with the officer.

A surge of alarm and concern swelled within him. Chelsea may be a con artist hiding a dangerous past, but if she was hurt, he didn't want her to refuse medical attention. He remembered how small she had looked, huddled in the backseat of the car, and how scared. A wave of protectiveness swept over him and warred with the frustration he was feeling. He asked the officer to wait a moment and waved the EMT back as he went over to the door where Chelsea was sitting.

"Don't you want them to make sure you're okay?"

"I know I'm okay physically. I'm just a little shaken up."

"That's not good enough. I want Miss Abigail to go in to the hospital for a thorough checkup, especially since she's scheduled for surgery in a couple of days." He paused and looked her in the eye. "You should go, as well."

Chelsea shook her head. "I'm fine, Mr. Sullivan. Thanks for asking, but short of a few bruises from the seat belt, I'm really okay."

"At least let them check your vital signs and give you a basic once-over. Okay?"

"Will you do the same? Your head has a nasty bump on it," Chelsea challenged.

Alex smiled. He didn't like doctors or getting medical attention any more than the next person, but if that's what it took for him to have peace of mind about her safety, he would do it. After the harrowing car chase, he wanted to be absolutely sure that she wasn't injured.

"Fine. It's a deal." He opened the car door and offered her his hand. She took it and allowed him to lead her to the EMT. It was a soft hand, with long feminine fingers, and he was actually hesitant to let go once the EMT began to work.

It wasn't long before the EMTs had completed their assessments on all three of them. While Chelsea had only a few bruises to report, the head technician had agreed that Miss Abigail and Alex needed a more thorough examination and he made the appropriate arrangements to take them in. Just as the three were about to get into the ambulance for the ride to the hospital, the trooper in charge of the scene approached.

"Well, we've already found the SUV. It was abandoned about ten miles down the road near a small restaurant. The owner reported it missing this morning. The driver is nowhere in sight, and none of the restaurant's customers remembered seeing anyone in a ball cap that fits your description the entire afternoon."

"What about fingerprints?" Alex asked.

The officer shook his head. "They'll check, but I wouldn't hold out much hope for any. It was probably just some drunk or meth head out joyriding and it got out of hand. We've had a couple of stolen cars lately, and the SUV is popular with a wild bunch that frequents a bar down the road."

"It was no drunk," Alex said forcefully. "The man driving was very deliberate with his attack, and he tried to kidnap Chelsea once our car was incapacitated. I believe it was the same man who had been watching the ladies at the observation deck."

The officer put up his hands in a motion of surrender. "Yes, sir, I was just saying it could have been a drunk. Don't worry. We'll do a thorough investigation." He turned to Chelsea.

"Did you get a good look at him, ma'am?"

She took a long time to answer, but finally whispered a response. "I was too scared to pay too much attention, but he was a big man, with dark eyes and dirty blond hair, just like Mr. Sullivan said."

The officer noted her response in a small spiral book. "Any distinguishing marks? A tattoo? Birthmark?"

"Not that I saw. I'm sorry, it just happened too fast for me to really notice, but he did smell like cigarette smoke."

Alex noticed the fatigue in Miss Abigail's eyes and knew it was time to get her to the hospital. Chelsea had done everything she could to comfort the elderly lady, but what Miss Abigail needed now was to get checked out and then get some rest from the traumatic morning.

The police agreed to contact the rental company and have their damaged car towed back to town. Alex knew it would be easy enough to get a taxi from the hospital to the hotel once Miss Abigail and he were given a clean bill of health. He helped the two ladies into the ambulance and said a silent prayer of thanks. It was truly by God's grace that they had survived without serious injury.

Despite the relief he felt, however, his mind was still filled with questions. Who was the maniac driving the SUV? Why had he attacked them? And what did the attack have to do with Chelsea's mysterious past?

Chelsea's heart broke as she helped settle Miss Abigail on the gurney in the ambulance. She was horri-

fied that she had put this sweet woman at risk. Despite
Alex's protests, the trooper still seemed convinced the
accident had been caused by a drug addict or a crazed
drunk, but Chelsea knew better. It had to have been
the man in the Braves cap, and he had to be working
with Carver. Who else would follow her to Maui from
Atlanta and stalk her every move? The only question
was, if it had been Carver's man, why hadn't the driver
just killed them all when he'd had the chance? And
why would he try to kidnap her? The entire event just
didn't make sense.

A wave of fear washed over her. What should she
do? If she stayed at the hotel with Miss Abigail, the
elderly woman and Alex's lives would be in danger
if—*when*—Carver's man tried to hurt Chelsea again.
If she left, then Miss Abigail's life would be in danger
during the operation if she experienced complications
and it was discovered they hadn't banked enough blood
to save her. The doctor had made it clear that Chelsea
needed to be close at hand both before and after the
surgery. Chelsea hugged herself and considered her options. Her meeting with the Southside business manager was tonight at eleven. She had to go—it was her
only hope of proving Carver's embezzlement and freeing herself from this nightmare. But if she stayed, was
there anything at all she could do to protect herself and
Miss Abigail from Carver's henchman?

She ran a hand through her hair and sighed. No
matter what she decided, she knew she couldn't depend upon anyone but herself. The men in her life had
always let her down and the police weren't dependable, either. Somehow, she needed to figure out what
to do to protect both herself and Miss Abigail before

this entire problem went any further. And what if the Southside business manager's documents didn't provide anything useful? What then?

She gave Miss Abigail's hand a reassuring squeeze. Somehow she was going to make it through this. All she had to do now was to figure out how.

SIX

Chelsea looked quickly to her right and left, then tried the door one more time. It was definitely locked. She looked up again at the decals plastered on the warehouse wall. It clearly stated that this was building 149. A huge sign also declared that Southside Renovations was the best source in Hawaii for copper building materials and native woods. She glanced at her watch. It was eleven o'clock on the dot. She was in the right place at the right time. So where was her contact?

Maybe there was another door somewhere on the building. She was hesitant to circle the large building in the dark since it was lit only by a distant, aging streetlight, but it didn't look as though she had much choice. A sinking feeling was slowly creeping into her stomach. She had tried to do her best to make sure she hadn't been followed, but she was quick to admit that she was no expert at playing cat and mouse with a kidnapper.

She stayed in the shadows as best she could, walking close to the side of the building as she looked for another door. Finally she found a back entrance under a small overhang. Just as she reached for the handle, a large bang sounded behind her. She jumped and flattened herself against the building, realizing quickly that there was nowhere to hide if someone truly wanted to hurt her. Had the Braves fan found her again?

A moment passed, then another. Then suddenly two stray dogs ran by. She looked carefully in the direction from where they had come and saw an old empty oil drum rolling near the wall of a nearby building. Apparently the dogs had knocked it over before running off, but the sound had taken at least ten years off her life at least. She put her hand on her heart and took a deep breath, trying to calm her nerves.

Once she was steady, she returned to the door and grabbed the knob. It turned easily in her hand and she sighed in relief. She'd just gone to the wrong door. That was it. Surely her contact was waiting for her inside with all of the documents she needed to send Carver to prison for good. Everything was fine. The car chase today had just made her jumpy, that's all.

The building was poorly lit, but she could make out rows of boxes to her right and several piles of rough building materials to her left. She headed toward a section that looked like an office. There was a light on inside the room that seeped under the closed door. Her contact had to be waiting for her in there.

She considered calling out for him, but the building was so eerily quiet that she held her tongue. As she approached the closed door, another thought occurred to her. Why hadn't he met her at the door, or at least been waiting for her someplace where she could easily find him? The whole scenario was causing her gut to twist in knots, but she couldn't stop now. Her objective was too important.

She opened the door and blinked rapidly as the light assaulted her eyes.

She screamed as the sight came into focus. A man's body lay limp across the desk. Blood from a visible head wound seeped over papers and files and dripped silently onto the floor, leaving a large puddle beneath the chair. It was so unnervingly similar to how she had found Roderick Carver that for a moment she felt as if she was back at Carver Enterprises, seeing her murdered boss all over again.

Slowly the differences became more apparent as the shock lessened. This man had brown hair instead of gray, and was wearing a Hawaiian shirt instead of the business suits that her boss had favored.

Suddenly a large hand covered her mouth as another hand grabbed her waist and pulled her back. She struggled against the grip and kicked and hit at her assailant, but nothing she did made him release his hold. If anything, his grip tightened. Whoever was holding her was big and very strong. One of her kicks hit the mark and the man grunted, but he still didn't release her. He pulled her out of the room and into the shadows of the main room of the warehouse.

"It's Alex," a masculine voice whispered, his breath hot against her neck. "Quit fighting me." He pulled her even farther away from the office. "If I take my hand off your mouth, will you promise not to scream anymore? I don't think we're alone in here."

Slowly, Chelsea nodded as his words registered. What was Alex doing here? Although she felt some measure of relief at his presence, she was also filled with questions.

"What are you…?"

"Shh," he hissed, again clamping his hand over her mouth. "They heard you scream and are coming to investigate. Keep quiet."

Two men came into view and she instantly understood. One was the man with the shaggy blond hair and the Braves cap. The other, skinnier with dark hair, wore a dark blue t-shirt and was equally menacing-looking. Both had guns drawn and were cautiously looking around, searching for their prey.

"Are you sure you heard something?" Blue Shirt asked.

"Yeah, I heard something all right."

"Well, I didn't see any cars parked outside. Where do you think she came from?"

Chelsea was instantly glad she'd taken a taxi to the warehouse district, and had asked the cabbie to drop her a few streets away from the building. She closed her eyes for a moment and said a prayer of thankfulness.

"How should I know?" Braves Cap replied roughly. "Let's check the street again. If she's seen the body, she probably already made a beeline outta here."

Blue Shirt agreed and the two headed to the door. A few seconds later Chelsea heard the door close behind them.

She breathed a sigh of relief and leaned into Alex's strength. He was still holding her around the waist and had pulled her closely against him. His arms were comforting, despite the circumstances. "What now?"

"Let's get out of here before they come back." He took her hand and led her to the door, then opened it slowly and peered outside, searching for any sign of the two men. Apparently seeing nothing, he pulled her behind him and together they sprinted away from the building. They hugged the shadows whenever they could and ran with all their might. After about a hundred yards or so he pulled her back against a building wall and listened, but there was no sound other than their own labored breathing.

"I don't think they're following us," she whispered, her chest heaving.

He nodded but didn't respond. She couldn't quite see his face in the shadows and wondered what he was thinking. Again, questions filled her mind.

"What were you doing there?" she asked quietly.

"Trying to figure you out," he whispered back. "I followed you once you left the hotel." He paused and there seemed to be a touch of anger in his voice mixed with alarm. "It's a good thing I did. You almost got yourself killed for the second time today."

For some irrational reason his attitude irritated her. "I could have handled it." Her words seemed silly even to her own ears, but she couldn't think of anything else to say.

"Well, now we're going to get somewhere safe and then we're going have a conversation, Chelsea Rogers. You're going to tell me what's going on once and for all." His voice left no room for argument and she shrank back a bit at his commanding tone.

He took her hand and they continued jogging in the shadows until they reached a silver SUV parked against the curb with rental car plates. He helped her into the passenger seat, then got in and drove away. The warehouse district disappeared behind them. Relief washed over her as she glanced behind the SUV and searched the street. No one was following them. She turned back around and focused on Alex. His body was rigid and his motions crisp. He didn't seem angry exactly, but he was definitely tense.

They drove for about ten minutes before Alex pulled over at a pay phone and dialed 9-1-1. Chelsea heard him report the murder. Afterward, they drove another half an hour along the highway in silence before Alex pulled the car off to the side of the road into an empty overlook and parked the car. He turned off the engine and the lights, and for a moment he just sat there, staring at the surf below them as it reflected the moonlight. When he turned to face her, she could see the concern in his eyes, mixed with frustration and trepidation.

"Okay, Chelsea. Are you ready to tell me what's going on?"

Chelsea shook her head. She had been dreading this conversation since they'd gotten in the car, but there hadn't been any way to dodge it. Her instinct was to avoid telling him anything that might lead him to discover her real identity, but at this point she wasn't sure that keeping her secret was still a realistic option. Dangerous men had already found her—was there any point in hiding her identity anymore? And was it really fair to keep him in the dark since her actions had put him and Miss Abigail in danger, as well? Still, telling Alex the entire truth tonight seemed like more than she could handle. Just the thought of sharing her past made her feel vulnerable and afraid.

Alex's fingers tightened on the steering wheel. "What's your real name, Chelsea? Let's start with that." He leaned closer, his voice a mere whisper in her ear. "I'm going to find out, you know. It may take me a few days, but sooner or later I'm going to discover what you're hiding. Why don't you save us both some time and enlighten me?"

Chelsea's lips thinned. She was so distressed that she barely seemed to notice when Alex reached for her hands and started rubbing them gently, his eyes still locked with hers. When he spoke, his voice was softer but still insistent. "Chelsea, Miss Abigail told me all about your Bombay blood. I've got my private investigator checking the blood registry as we speak, not to mention immigration records and other sources. I'm going to find out who you really are." He paused. "It's my job to protect my client. I don't know what you're involved in, but somebody tried to kill us today, and I just pulled you out of a building with a dead body in it. It's time to end the secrets. Whatever this is has gone way too far."

Chelsea's heart was thumping against her chest and it felt heavy inside her. She realized that her breath was coming in gasps so she tried to slow things down and steady her nerves. What was she supposed to do? Could she trust him? She said a silent prayer for guidance and then tried to pull her hands away but Alex refused to release her. In fact, the more she pulled, the tighter he held her.

"Talk to me, Chelsea. Tell me what you're hiding. I'm a fairly good attorney, you know. If you've gotten in over your head with something, I promise I'll do what I can to help you."

"Why do you keep pushing?" she asked, her voice barely above a whisper. "Why can't you just let it go?"

"Have you been listening to me at all?" His eyes flashed. "Because we were almost killed today. Because that man tried to kidnap you on the road. Because we just ran away from a warehouse with a corpse in it, and two men were looking for you with loaded weapons. I can't stop now until I find out the truth." He softened his voice. "I guess the bottom line is that I'm worried about you. You're in trouble and I want to help, but I can't do that unless you tell me what's going on."

"You can't help. Nobody can." She suddenly jerked her hands free, yanked open the door and started running away from the SUV. She didn't get far. Alex ran after her and grabbed her arm, stopping her retreat. When he spoke, his voice was gentle, and the tenderness she heard was almost her undoing.

"Look, I know you're scared. I don't understand why, but I really want to. I want to help you with whatever it is that you're running from. Please, let me."

Chelsea pulled against his grip, but knew she could never break free. He wasn't hurting her, but he wasn't letting go, either. She finally stopped but wouldn't meet his eyes. She looked out at the waves instead.

"Don't you think I want to tell you? I just can't. It's too dangerous. The past two days should have convinced you of that. I've been foolish for not leaving already. I don't want you or Miss Abigail to get dragged into the middle of things and get hurt because of me."

"We're already in the middle, wouldn't you say?"

Chelsea bit her bottom lip and looked as if she was about to cry. "I have to leave. I've already stayed longer than I should have. I have to get away from Maui as soon as I possibly can."

SEVEN

"Why?" Alex asked softly, hoping and praying that this time she'd finally give him the answers he needed to help her. "Who is the violent man with unlimited resources that is chasing you?"

Chelsea's eyes widened in surprise. "Miss Abigail told you?"

Alex nodded. "I kind of pried it out of her, but yes, she did, although she didn't know much. She thinks you were the victim of domestic violence. Is that true?"

Chelsea closed her eyes. A moment passed and she chewed her bottom lip again, then took a deep breath and met his eyes. "When I was a child, yes, but that's not what's going on now."

Alex could see the distress on her face and wished he could erase her pain, but there was simply no way to do so. If she could only trust him with her story, he could help her sort through the mess. He took her hand and led her over to the rock wall that separated the parking area from the beach below and they sat on the wall, facing each other. "Well?"

She squeezed his hands. "Ever heard of Justin Carver?"

Alex's brow furrowed. "Vaguely. I think he's one of the movers and shakers in Chicago. Is that right?"

Chelsea nodded. "Yes, that's the one. I used to work for his father. Justin took over the family's real-estate business when his father died."

Alex frowned. "What does he have to do with this?"

Chelsea squeezed his hand. "A couple of months ago, I was working in Chicago as an accountant for his father, Roderick Carver. We discovered Justin had been siphoning off large sums of money from the company into his own personal accounts. One night, we were going over the numbers one last time, and I left to get some coffee. When I came back, I found Justin standing over his father's body, smoke still coming out of the barrel of the gun." She swallowed at the memory. "There was so much blood!" She gestured at the scar on her cheek. "He tried to kill me, too, but I escaped with this little reminder from his bullet."

She took a deep breath and forged steadily on. "Justin Carver is a very powerful and dangerous man—and he knew who I was, knew my name and my face. Thanks to the employee records, he knew my address and who I had listed as my emergency contact. After the murder I couldn't even go back to my apartment because I knew he and his thugs would be waiting for me there.

"I cleaned out my bank account, bought a fake driver's license and caught the next flight to Tallahassee. I remembered hearing that somebody on the Bombay blood registry had placed an ad promising to pay a small amount for someone with Bombay blood if they could come to Tallahassee and be available during the operation. As long as I had to start over somewhere,

I figured I might as well be somewhere that I could help someone and earn a little money at the same time. That's how I found Miss Abigail. I offered to help her bank the blood she needed for her operation, but we hit it off so well that she ended up offering me the companion job."

Alex considered her words. "What did the police do about Roderick's murder?"

Chelsea shrugged. "Nothing that I know of. The news reported that Roderick Carver committed suicide." She hugged herself nervously. "That's why Justin is trying to kill me. I'm the only one that isn't on his payroll who knows differently—and who knows about the embezzlement." She paused. "When his father died, Justin inherited a huge amount of money, and he was able to use it to cover up the holes in the company's books. He also must have made the murder look like a suicide. His original plan was to frame me for the embezzlement and then make it look as though his father had killed me and then himself. I guess he thought he'd benefit more by covering up the embezzlement so his money laundering could continue, rather than exposing the theft and blaming me.

"Roderick was very tight with his books, and wouldn't discuss them with anyone but me. Once I was out of the picture, there was no one else who knew anything about the theft or the murder. Now all Justin has to do is kill me and he'll get away scot-free with all of his crimes. I'm the only thing standing between him and the potential of a life sentence in prison."

Alex shook his head. Everything she said was making sense. It all fit with what he already knew about her; her lack of a past in the public records and her furtive answers whenever he had tried to dig a little deeper to discover the truth. No wonder she had been so elusive! She had been guarding her life and her safety. A wave of guilt swept over him as he remembered the distrustful way he had treated Chelsea from day one. Apparently she had never been after Miss Abigail's money, but was really only there to help the woman through the surgery, as she'd claimed. Still, the sheer magnitude of her statements stunned him. He had expected a jilted boyfriend or even someone she had robbed in some penny-ante scheme, not a murder cover-up.

"How do you think they found you?"

Chelsea shrugged but emotion flooded her features and she started to cry. "I don't have the faintest idea. I found a note in my purse on the plane to Maui that said 'I know who you are,' but nothing in it mentioned Chicago or my real name. I thought—I guess I wanted to think it wasn't connected, that it was just a cruel joke or a prank." She let a sob escape. "I didn't want to believe that the danger followed me to Maui, but now I know that the car attack was because of me. Carver must have sent that man in the baseball cap to kidnap me." She sucked in a breath, trying to stay in control, but another sob got away from her. "I was trying to do the right thing by being here for Miss Abigail during her surgery, but all I did was put you both in danger. I'm so sorry!"

Alex shook his head. "Shh. It's okay. You did the right thing. Miss Abigail needed you here, and she still does." He gently rubbed his thumb over the back of her hand. "There's still one thing I don't understand, though. Why didn't you just go to the police in Chicago and tell them what happened?"

"I don't trust them. When I was a teenager, my father had an alcohol problem, and used to beat up my mom. When she called the police, they wouldn't do anything, and then my father would take his anger out on me. They got separated and eventually divorced. When my mom told the judge about the abuse, he didn't believe either one of us and forced me to continue visiting my dad until I turned eighteen. Usually the police had to handle the transfer, and even though they saw the bruises, they did nothing.

"After all of that, I figured the cops would never believe me over the word of Justin Carver. Justin is a very wealthy man with connections all over Chicago, and he'd already told me that he was going to blame me for the embezzlement and the murder. I just couldn't take that chance."

Alex mulled over everything she was telling him. "What about the man at the warehouse? Why were you there? What does that have to do with Carver?"

Chelsea shook her head. "I decided that if I could prove Justin embezzled the funds, then I'd have hard evidence against him—more than just my word against his. Then maybe I could convince the police to believe me. So I did some research. I found out that Justin was using a company called Southside Renovations to launder his money, and they just happen to have their corporate headquarters in Maui. The dead man was the company's business manager who had agreed to let me examine their books and give me copies of their audits. Southside seems to be a legitimate company, and he didn't like the idea of being used by Justin Carver any more than I did. I was supposed to meet him tonight at eleven to get the documents, but I doubt there's anything to find now. I'm sure that whoever got to the business manager first destroyed whatever he was going to give me. Now I'm back to square one." She stood abruptly. "I have to leave. I have to just grab my things and disappear tonight. I've already put you and Miss Abigail in too much danger."

Alex didn't know what the future held, but he did know one thing—he wasn't ready for Chelsea to disappear. A wave of compassion and protectiveness swept over him. He motioned to the ledge. "Please sit back down."

She hesitated, but finally seated herself again, her expression reluctant. He leaned in close, until his face was just a few inches away and his breath brushed against her skin.

"You can't leave. I got a call today from the clinic with some bad news. I know you've been banking blood for a month now, but the storage facility had a temperature malfunction and some of their supply was compromised—including all the blood you sent ahead. I spoke to the doctor and they believe they've fixed the problem, but he said that he really didn't want to bank more blood and then run the risk of it becoming unusable, as well. He also didn't want to tap you dry. He said it was safer for Miss Abigail if we just wait until the day of the surgery and have you immediately available if a transfusion becomes necessary."

Her face fell and immediately showed her distress. "All of it was ruined?"

"Yes. I'm sorry." He paused a moment, letting the news sink in, then reached over and touched Chelsea's chin, gently raising her head so that he could see her large brown eyes. They were wide and troubled. "Please don't run, Chelsea. More than ever, Miss Abigail needs you to be in Maui when she goes to the hospital." He swallowed. "I can keep you safe until then. Let me help you. Please. I'm a lawyer and I have connections. Trust me. I promise I'll do all I can to help you."

Chelsea chewed her bottom lip, uncertainty painted across her features.

Alex felt his stomach grip in fear. She was going to leave, and he was never going to see her again. He could see it in her eyes. He didn't know why the thought bothered him so much, but right now wasn't the time to analyze his feelings. He had to think of something fast. "Look, we can work through this. I can call the doctor again and make sure they've considered every possible option." He paused, knowing he was only postponing the inevitable. "We can call the police—"

"No police!" Chelsea said quickly. "Not until I have proof."

After what she had revealed, Alex wasn't surprised. "Okay. No police. I can hire a bodyguard tonight, and we can alert hotel security. Tomorrow I'll help you start researching this and we'll come up with a plan of action. I'm thinking if we can somehow get a forensic accountant to go over Carver's books, we can find the embezzlement. We just have to figure out a way to get access to the company computer systems." He smiled for the first time tonight. "We can get through this— together. And, think of Miss Abigail. She needs you to be here during the surgery. That's why you came to Hawaii in the first place, right?"

She didn't answer him so he pushed forward. "Please. I'll keep you safe. I promise."

"This isn't all about me," Chelsea whispered. "Everyone around me is in danger."

Alex gripped her hands again. "Stay until Miss Abigail's surgery, Chelsea. That's all I'm asking. Please, give me a chance to help."

There was still a look of distress on her face, but finally she nodded. "Okay, Alex. If you get Miss Abigail a bodyguard and let the hotel know about the man with the Braves cap, then I'll stay until Miss Abigail's operation. But then I'm gone."

EIGHT

Chelsea unwrapped the plush rose-pink chenille robe and held it out to Miss Abigail who was sitting on the bed, a large smile on her face. "Oh, it's so beautiful!"

Chelsea smiled back. "It's really soft, and the color will look gorgeous on you. Are you sure you like it?"

The older woman took it and ran her aged hand over the collar. "It's perfect!" she said. "I can't believe how soft the fabric is. It's just what I needed. I'm going to wear it right now as I go down to the spa for my appointment. I'm having Terme Wailea hydrotherapy. Have you heard of it?"

Chelsea shook her head so Ms. Abigail reached for the brochure on the desk and started reading. "'Purifying and invigorating in nature, this therapy allows you to rest amid calming bubbles in a Japanese Furo bath. It's a memorable and luxurious spa experience.'" She paused and sighed. "Doesn't it just sound wonderful? I'll probably feel like I'm nineteen again!"

"I'm sure you'll enjoy it," Chelsea said with a smile just as she heard a knock on the door. "You'll be so relaxed when you come back you won't ever want to go back home to Tallahassee."

Ms. Abigail winked at her. "I'm counting on it. I plan on luxuriating in there all day." She thumbed through the brochure one more time. "You know, there's still time for you to go with me to enjoy the spa…" She raised her eyebrow hopefully but Chelsea shook her head right before she peeked through the peephole and then opened the door to let Alex enter the room.

"Hello, Mr. Sullivan."

Alex raised an eyebrow. "That's a bit formal, isn't it?"

Chelsea shrugged, still feeling a bit unsure about her relationship with Alex and her decision to stay in Maui. She had given him a modicum of trust, but wasn't ready to trust him completely or to do anything that would make her too dependent upon him or his offer of help.

She nodded at Mr. Westin, the bodyguard Alex had hired to oversee their safety for the duration of their stay in Hawaii. He was stationed outside their door and had promised to keep outsiders away and to watch for the men they had seen at the warehouse. The hotel had also promised to station a security officer at the spa as well as in any other section of the hotel they cared to visit.

Alex and Chelsea hadn't given Miss Abigail much explanation for hiring Mr. Westin, but after the car attack it hadn't been that hard to convince her to hire some security and to take a few extra precautions. Alex's investigator had sung praises about Mr. Westin, and the man was free for a week to stand guard at Miss Abigail's room both now and after the surgery, as well. So far Mr. Westin had said next to nothing, but he was big and intimidating and, most importantly, he had passed Alex's scrutiny during the interview.

"Please come to the spa with me, Chelsea," Miss Abigail entreated. "I promise you'll enjoy it."

"I appreciate your offer, Ms. Abigail, but spa treatments have never been my thing."

"She needs to go with me anyway," Alex interjected. "We're going to head to downtown Kahului to do some research in a little while."

Miss Abigail's face instantly registered distress. "Will you be safe? Maybe you should take Mr. Westin with you."

"I'll protect Chelsea," Alex stated in a matter-of-fact tone. "I want Mr. Westin to stay here with you." Although Chelsea was the one who was courting danger, Alex wasn't so sure that the man in the Braves cap wouldn't stoop to kidnapping Miss Abigail to get his hands on Chelsea. He would feel much more comfortable if Mr. Westin kept an eye on Miss Abigail at the hotel while he did the same with Chelsea while they were out.

"Well, if you're sure," Miss Abigail said lightly. She patted Chelsea on the back, smiled and then opened the door and took Mr. Westin's arm. "Take care of her, Alex." With a wink and a nod, the two disappeared down the hallway.

Alex watched her go, shaking his head in amusement. The elderly woman was handling everything that had happened with amazing grace and fortitude.

He set up his laptop on the desk and pulled up a second chair. "Ready to see what research we can handle from here?"

Chelsea nodded and joined him with her own laptop. She clicked on the site for Southside Renovations and navigated through the various pages, telling Alex what she knew about the company and her relationship with the business manager as they scrolled through the different sections. Neither spotted anything unusual about the company.

"Do you remember the names of any of the other construction companies Carver used for his real-estate repairs?" Alex asked.

"A couple." She directed him to the sites of the other companies and they scoured the pages, but couldn't find anything unusual on those sites, either. Justin Carver's name was never mentioned, but then, Alex didn't really expect the connection to be that readily apparent. Still, they'd had to start somewhere, and familiarizing himself with the players in the case seemed like a good way to begin.

He snuck a look at Chelsea, who was typing furiously on her keyboard, and couldn't deny he was struggling with his feelings about her. On the one hand, he knew she still wasn't being completely honest with him. In fact, even though she had told him quite a bit last night, he realized he still didn't even know her real name. On the other hand, ever since the car chase on the mountainside, he had been feeling a need to protect her and to ensure her safety. He still couldn't explain the conflicting feelings warring within him, and when she turned and motioned for him to notice something on her screen, he pushed the thoughts away and gave her his full attention.

"Was there anything unusual about Justin's behavior in the office? Anything that would help us know what to look for?" he asked.

Chelsea shrugged. "Justin was never especially productive at work, but he used to spend hours there on the weekends and when others were out on vacation. It made him look as though he was sincerely devoted to the job, but now I wonder if he was just spending that time altering documents and covering up his embezzlement trail while no one was watching."

Alex made a few notes on details he thought might be important from the various sites and then leaned back in his chair. "What we need is that last audit you saw of Carver Enterprises. Do you think any copies of the original even still exist?"

"I doubt it." Chelsea answered. "Surely he's altered it by now to cover up his theft."

Alex ran his fingers through his hair. "We have to somehow find a copy. Or, better yet, to access the company records so we can get a forensic accountant to conduct an audit of the books. No matter what people do to cover their tracks, those forensic techs are amazing at following the bread crumbs. Since they're specifically trained to look for fraud, forensic accountants can sometimes gather evidence and discover problems that wouldn't raise any red flags during a normal audit. I've also heard that forensic computer experts can follow someone's keystroke tracks and in many cases, recover deleted or hidden files with the right program."

Chelsea nodded. "I agree, but in order to get to any of that, we'd have to have access to Carver's hard drive on his laptop. The man does all of his work on one computer that he constantly carries around with him, and if there's something to be found, that's where the evidence will be hidden."

Alex snapped his fingers. "I'm not a computer expert, but maybe there's a way to access his hard drive remotely without Justin even realizing it." His fingers flew over the keyboard and a moment later he was showing her a website that advertised excellent pattern-matching software. He made some more notes and then searched for and found a couple of other file-extraction mechanisms that would pull out and analyze any interesting data within set parameters from Justin's files.

He leaned back in his chair again. "All we need now is access. We can purchase one of these programs, remotely connect to Carver's laptop through the internet, have it download the files we need from Carver's computer and then hire a forensic accountant and computer specialist to analyze them for us. I'm sure we can find the proof we're looking for if we can just get our hands on those files."

"But how do we connect to Carver's laptop?"

"Tony D'Angelo, my private investigator, has a way, I'm sure of it. He's something of a computer genius."

Chelsea smiled. "If we can get those files, then Justin will end up in prison for sure." Without taking time to think, she leaned over, grasped Alex's hand and squeezed it, then quickly let go. "Thank you for helping me. I can't tell you how much I appreciate it. I had pretty much given up hope last night after what happened at the warehouse."

It was the first time she had initiated any physical contact with him and the action surprised him. Alex felt a warmth fill his chest that he hadn't expected. He stood and offered her his hand to pull her up from her chair. "Ready to go downtown and see what we can find in the public records?" She nodded and let him pull her gently to her feet. When she stood, they were only inches apart. They paused there for a moment, their eyes locked. A jolt of electricity seemed to shoot between them before Chelsea quickly stepped back. She looked around nervously and awkwardly slipped on her sandals.

"Sure, let's go."

Chelsea and Alex got into the rental car and made the trip across the island without saying a word, but unlike last night, it was a comfortable silence. Once they made it to Kahului, they used the SUV's GPS system to locate the business registration division of the Department of Commerce and Consumer Affairs. The government agency allowed people to search for basic information through their online database, but for more detailed corporate records, a person had to come down and pay a fee at the state office. Neither Alex nor Chelsea was convinced they'd find much, but they had to start somewhere, and the business regulation office was the best place to begin their research. If they found a connection to Carver buried in the paperwork, then the risk of leaving the safety of the hotel would definitely be worth it.

Chelsea glanced at Alex out of the corner of her eye as they entered the building and made their way to the counter. She couldn't believe he had gone so quickly from being an adversary to an ally, but she felt trust slowly beginning to form between them despite the rough beginning of their fragile relationship. Every time she had trusted a man in her past, it had caused pain and suffering. Would Alex be the one to break the cycle? Only time would tell, but at least she was cautiously willing to give him a chance.

A short forty-five minutes later they had copies of the incorporation papers of three separate businesses that Chelsea thought might have ties to Carver Enterprises, including Southside Renovations. There was nothing readily apparent in the paperwork to tie the companies together, but Chelsea hoped that if they actually got access to Carver's computer, they could run a variety of searches with Alex's program that would connect the dots for them.

Suddenly Alex grabbed her hand and roughly pulled her to a crouching position behind a black Ford pickup. "It's the Braves fan," Alex hissed, motioning to his right. "He must have followed us, which means he knows what car we're driving."

"If he followed us, why didn't he come inside the office? We've been in there almost an hour."

Alex shrugged. "Who knows? Maybe he was waiting for us to come out and when he didn't see us for such a long time, decided to go in and check. Or maybe he got a call from Carver that kept him busy. Whatever the reason, he's here now and we need to find another way out of here."

A shiver of fear swept over her. Would that man never stop? She glanced over the hood of the pickup and could see Braves Cap walking toward the building they had just exited. He was wearing a blue polo shirt and jeans, dark sunglasses that hid his eyes and of course, the telltale red-and-blue Braves cap. She looked quickly around, inspiration hitting her as she noticed a sign by the road.

"The Queen Ka'ahumanu Center is only one block away, and it's sure to be full of people. Maybe we can lose him in there and then catch a taxi back to the hotel.

Mr. Westin and the hotel security team can deal with him from there."

Alex nodded. "Good idea." They continued to use the parked cars along the roadside as cover until they reached the mall, running the last few yards when no further protection existed between the parking lot and the mall doors.

The Queen Ka'ahumanu Center was the largest mall on the island. It wasn't as big as the Governor's Square Mall back in Tallahassee, but it did offer a large variety of stores, a small food court and even a farmer's market where locals sold fresh vegetables and fruit. It was fairly crowded and Chelsea said a short prayer of thanks. Hopefully they'd be able to blend in with the other customers and escape their pursuer before he could approach them.

Chelsea looked over her shoulder on several occasions, but didn't see her adversary. Still, she couldn't relax as they walked and her hands wouldn't stop shaking.

"Pretend we're just a couple of tourists," Alex said as he gently took her hand. "We'll be less conspicuous."

They walked a bit farther and then Alex gently led her into a store on their right. While many of the shops were filled with Hawaiian tourist paraphernalia, this store was set up more like an art gallery. The displays were filled with beautiful dishes, boxes and other furniture intricately carved out of Koa wood, a native material with shimmering highlights that changed as the wood caught the light. She took a deep breath and tried to settle her nerves by focusing on the items offered for sale. The prices made her gasp, but she had truly never seen anything lovelier. She looked up at Alex, who was clearly keeping an eye on the shoppers around them.

The shop owner followed them around for a few minutes, obviously hoping to talk them into a sale, but he eventually left them alone after Alex insisted they were just admiring the craftsmanship and wouldn't be buying today. Suddenly she felt Alex squeeze her hand and she met his eyes, instantly alert.

His eyes darted to the left and she quickly turned her head to see what had caught his attention. The Braves fan was outside the store, across the hallway of the mall.

Fear gripped her as he stared at her, clearly aware that he had found his prey. His lips curved into a smile as he crossed his arms and leaned against the wall as if he was settling in to watch her. He ignored Alex completely as if he wasn't even there.

"What are we going to do?" she whispered.

"Keep walking," Alex said quietly. He patted her hand as if nothing was wrong, nodded to the storekeeper and led her into the crowd. They walked a short distance and she dared a look behind her. Her stalker had fallen in about thirty feet behind them. He noticed her backward glance and gave her a large wicked grin in response, filled with menace. Her heart beat frantically against her chest as fear swam within her. She squeezed Alex's arm and walked even faster.

"Keep your eye open for mall security," Alex murmured. He pulled out his cell phone and handed it to Chelsea, then quickly turned and headed toward the man. "Call the police. I'm going after him."

"No!" Chelsea said as she grabbed his arm. "I think I saw a gun in his waistband."

Alex pulled his arm away and looked Chelsea straight in the eye. "It'll be okay. Call the police. I can handle this."

Chelsea raced around him and got in his way. "Do you want to bet your life on that? He could shoot you and disappear into this crowd before anyone could stop him."

Alex looked over at the Braves fan who was still a good thirty feet away. There was still a wall of people between the two, but Alex caught the man's eye and the man smiled at him with a sinister grin. Then he pointed his finger at Alex as though it was a gun and made a firing motion with his thumb. After the shot, he blew on his finger as if it were smoking, then laughed and started moving toward them.

Chelsea never got to call 9-1-1. She pocketed the phone as Alex grabbed her arm and they started running, darting around tourists and ignoring the stunned shoppers' protests that they bumped along the way as they tried to escape their pursuer. Her breath came in gasps and she lost both sandals, but she kept running, doing her best to stay close to Alex as he darted around the people and vendors in the walkway.

They heard a loud crash and Chelsea dared a look behind her. The Braves fan had apparently tried to leap over an empty chair that one of the vendors had been using, but his foot had caught the top of it and pushed the chair violently into the cart, which had overturned. Yelling and other noise ensued, but Chelsea turned and continued her escape.

* * *

They ran until they reached one of the larger anchor stores and entered quickly through the men's department. Alex suddenly pulled her to the side behind a rack of blue jeans. "I think I see him."

Chelsea's eyes grew wide but she moved behind him and scrunched against the wall. Out of the corner of his eye, Alex saw her wrap her arms around her waist and hold her breath.

A moment passed, then another. Just as Alex was about to step out to see if the man was anywhere in sight, the Braves fan passed about twenty feet in front of them without looking in their direction. Alex got a better look at the man as he walked by, and he could even catch the scent of body odor and cigar smoke. He looked back at Chelsea whose skin had turned a pasty-white and a wave of protectiveness swept over him. She met his eyes and he gave her a reassuring smile. Somehow they were going to make it through this, and he was going to do whatever he needed to do to keep her safe. A metallic click made him freeze in the middle of his thought.

"Isn't it fun when a cat-and-mouse game comes to an end and the cat devours the mouse?"

NINE

Alex turned to see the Braves fan standing not two feet away from them and pointing a pistol directly at Chelsea. He slowly moved between the gun and Chelsea, but the man only smiled.

"Do you really think you're going to stop me from taking her?"

Chelsea gasped at his words, but Alex's tone didn't waiver. "Absolutely. She's not going anywhere with you."

The man laughed. "Well, you see, that's where you're wrong. She has a date with a friend of mine, and I'm here to escort her." He took a step to the side to get a better look at his prey. Alex moved, as well, shielding Chelsea as best he could. The man laughed again. "In case you haven't noticed, I'm the one with the gun here. Give her to me now without making any more of a scene and I'll let you live."

Suddenly, Chelsea threw a pile of T-shirts at the man, hitting the hand holding the gun. It wasn't much of a distraction, but while the gun went off, the shot went wild. She and Alex both ducked as the bullet missed them both and shattered a nearby mannequin's head instead.

Alex saw his chance to strike and hit the man's wrist with such a fierce blow that the pistol went flying. He then hit the man square in the jaw. The Braves fan staggered back a couple of steps but recovered quickly and launched himself at Alex, catching him around the waist as Chelsea darted out of the way. The momentum pushed the two men crashing into a display table filled with stacks of shorts and shirts, toppling the mannequin. Alex brought his knee up and slammed it into the man's chin. The Braves fan's grip loosened as he fell to the floor. He took a moment to recover, then stood and charged Alex again, this time catching Alex's gut with a punch of his own.

Before Alex could catch his breath, a second punch caught his bottom lip and he felt the blood start dripping down his chin. Alex groaned and staggered back, but didn't fall until he was tackled to the floor. The two men rolled a couple of times as they wrestled for supremacy, but then the assailant got in a couple of good punches and ended up straddling Alex. "I hope you're not too attached to those pretty teeth of yours," the man said viciously as he raised his fist.

Alex put up his arm to shield the blow, but flinched at the sound of a loud crack. He felt the man's weight shift and looked up in surprise.

Chelsea stood behind them, the mannequin's arm still in her hands. She'd used it like a club to hit the Braves fan in the head. The ball cap went flying as the man fell to the side, but the blow hadn't been hard enough to knock him out completely.

She raised the arm to hit him again, but he had recovered quickly and was ready for the second blow. With a speed Alex had never seen before, the man wrenched the club from Chelsea's hands and then pulled himself to his feet.

"So you want to play, too, princess? That's just fine with me. My boss doesn't care what condition you're in, as long as I deliver you alive." He tossed the mannequin arm aside and advanced on her, still smiling, a look of pure evil on his face.

"Freeze all of you!"

Alex looked over to see a security guard only a few feet away approaching slowly with his weapon drawn. The red laser light from the front of the Taser swung back and forth between the two men's chests.

"All right, get your hands up and step back." The mall cop motioned with his hand and Alex stood, his hands raised.

The Braves fan seemed to be complying, too—but then he made a dive for the gun that had been knocked aside earlier in the fight. Before he could fire, however, a buzz of electric current snaked across the air.

Alex flinched involuntarily as his gaze flew to the young security guard whose eyes were wide, the Taser still in his hand. Alex turned back toward his attacker just in time to see him fall to his knees. The two probes were attached to his chest and the electricity surged through his body, making the man appear as if he was having a seizure. Braves Cap gritted his teeth and fell the rest of the way to the floor, then curled up in a ball, totally incapacitated. Utter surprise and pain registered on his face.

Alex caught his breath for a minute. Was this really happening? He had never seen someone use a Taser before, and from the look on the security guard's face, the experience was rather new to him, also. He slowly lowered his hands. As the guard approached and quickly handcuffed the Braves fan, Alex rushed to Chelsea's side and pulled her against his chest to shield her from the view. She was crying and couldn't seem to stop.

Chelsea grabbed on to Alex and buried her face against his chest, the sheer magnitude of the events causing her head to feel as if it was spinning out of control. If Alex hadn't been with her today, the man would have kidnapped her and gift-wrapped her for Carver. It was as simple as that.

She felt her legs shaking and was grateful when Alex led her over to one of the ruined displays and helped her to sit before sitting beside her. He put his arm around her and pulled her close and she leaned into his embrace. The man obviously worked for Carver, but his arrest didn't mean she was safe. Was Carver already on the island? How many others had he sent to hunt her down?

"How are you doing?" Alex asked softly as he brushed the hair away from her face. "Are you hanging in there?"

"You saved my life," she whispered in response. She pulled back and looked him in the eye, seeing compassion and strength staring back at her. "Thank you."

"You're very welcome," Alex said as he gave her a reassuring squeeze. "The police will be here soon and you'll have to tell them what's going on."

She tensed at his words. Of course the police would come. In the heat of the moment she hadn't even considered the ramifications of what had just happened. "I can't tell them much. I still don't have the proof I need to send Carver to prison. If I make any accusations against him without solid proof, I know he'll find a way to turn it around on me and I'll be the one who ends up in prison. We can't let the police know what's really happened until we have evidence against him they can't ignore."

Alex paused a moment, as if considering her words, then nodded. "Okay, Chelsea. We'll tell them the bare minimum for now."

Chelsea realized she had been holding her breath, waiting to hear if Alex would support her plan or not. A huge part of her expected him to ignore her plea and insist on telling the police everything, but she was pleasantly surprised at his support. It was the first time that she could remember a man in her life backing her up and believing in her. The fledgling trust she felt for him grew a little stronger.

She turned her thoughts back to the authorities. Would the police discover her true identity in the process of their investigation? They hadn't pressed yesterday after the assault in the car, but two attacks in two days would undoubtedly raise some red flags.

A knot tightened in her stomach. Between the police, Carver and whoever Carver had hired aside from the Braves fan, there was no way she could be safe in Maui anymore. She had to leave. She hated to put Miss Abigail's health in peril during the operation, but Carver wouldn't stop until she was dead, and she really had no choice. She would return to the hotel with Alex after the police allowed them to leave, but tonight after Alex and Miss Abigail were asleep, she would pack her things and disappear.

* * *

"Oh, my!" Miss Abigail's eyes were wide and filled with concern. "Are you sure you're okay?"

Alex took a sip from his coffee and tossed his tie on the table. "Yes, Miss Abigail. It has been a harrowing two days, but I'm just fine. The police have promised to call if anything breaks in the case. They believe, and I agree, that the man they captured at the mall was the same one who attacked us on the road yesterday. I must admit, I feel a lot safer now knowing he's behind bars."

"Why was he chasing us?" she asked, her eyes wide.

"The police are trying to find that out, but he's not being very forthcoming," Alex responded, mindful of his promise not to share Chelsea's secrets.

"You should know, Alex," Miss Abigail said with a pat on his hand as she took a seat, "how glad I am that you're in Hawaii with us and were there to protect Chelsea when she needed you. I know you hadn't really planned on coming with us to Maui, and I had no idea that you would end up fighting a villain on this trip and that your life would be at risk! Now that this nastiness is behind us, maybe you can relax a bit and take a well-deserved vacation."

She gave him a conspirator's smile. "I'm glad you're getting to know Chelsea better. She really is a very sweet lady with a lot to offer. I was hoping something might develop between you two. I think you and Chelsea would make a great couple. I know you haven't been looking for romance after what happened last time, but she's so beautiful and kind, and just a perfect fit for you...."

Taking a seat opposite her, Alex shook his head. "My last relationship crashed and burned, Miss Abigail. I'm not really ready to try again—not with anyone." He sat back in his chair, thinking about Chelsea despite his words. He knew that she was different from Irene. His former fiancée would never have done something as selfless as giving blood to a stranger. And he couldn't help remembering how Chelsea had looked with that mannequin arm in her hand, fighting the Braves fan to protect Alex. She'd been clearly terrified, but she hadn't run or even just stood by. She'd rushed in to help him. Not in a million years would Irene have done something like that.

Still, he wasn't ready to open himself up to the potential pain involved with a serious relationship.

"Maybe," admitted Miss Abigail, "but you've been stuck in your legal files so long, I don't think you truly realize that life is passing you by."

"That's my choice," Alex said adamantly.

"You're right, of course." Miss Abigail nodded. "I have no business meddling in your personal life." She stood and came to stand right in front of him, her head tilted so she could meet his eyes. "But I've been around eighty-three years, and I actually know a thing or two. I know that you've pulled away from God, and that your job has become your life." She poked him on the shoulder with her finger. "If you don't change the way you're living, you're going to end up alone and with a chest full of regrets."

A muscle jumped in Alex's jaw, but he silently mulled over her words. Miss Abigail reached out and cupped his face with her hand, her aged skin soft against his cheek. When he caught her eye he saw only love and devotion staring back at him.

"Please forgive an old woman for meddling. I don't

usually hatch matchmaking schemes, but I care about you, Alex. I'd like to think we've been more than client and attorney all of these years. I'd like to call you my friend, and as your friend, I have to admit, I'm saddened by the way you live your life." A tear glistened in her eye. "I hope you can make a change or two before your work consumes you."

Alex stood and put his hands on his hips. He wanted to be angry at her for criticizing his choices, but in the end, he couldn't blame her for voicing her concerns. He knew Miss Abigail had acted out of kindness and worry for him, and he couldn't fault her for her attempts to save him from himself.

He shook his head. "I'm not sure that I agree with you, but I will admit that you've given me quite a bit to think about." He reached out and squeezed her hand. "You're more than just a friend, Miss Abigail. You have to know I love you like family."

As if on cue, Chelsea walked through the door with a bucket of ice and two sodas in her hands. "They were out of lemon-lime, Miss Abigail, so I got you a Dr Pepper. I hope that's okay."

She poured the soda into a glass, added some ice and brought the drink over to the elderly lady who was now sitting near the sliding-glass door that led to the balcony. "Alex, did you want anything?"

Before he could answer, his cell phone buzzed. It was his investigator. He shook his head, then waved goodbye as he went through the door to his adjoining room.

"Sully? Tony. You got a few minutes?"

Alex took a seat in the desk chair and leaned back,

cradling the cell phone as he did so. "Sure. What've you got?"

Tony cleared his throat. "Well, it's like this. I've finally got a lead on your mysterious lady in Hawaii."

Alex's pulse seemed to increase and he leaned forward. Chelsea had stuck with her fake name throughout the police interviews this afternoon, and although she had shared quite a bit about her past, he still wanted to know more. "That's great news. What have you found?"

"Well, Chelsea Rogers is definitely an alias. I ran her prints and she popped up in the Illinois family court database."

"Family court?"

"Yeah, that's right. Her real name is Cecilia Eliana Rigo. She's twenty-seven, and really did move to the U.S. from Brazil when she was twelve. Apparently she got stuck in the middle of a very nasty divorce between her mother and father during her teenage years and there were serious allegations of physical abuse by the father. There must not have been enough proof of the abuse to satisfy the judge, though, because he ordered visitation with the father despite the mother's testimony. The mother refused to comply with the judge's order, and was held in contempt of court twice. The police got involved several times in the custody transfer, and Cecilia was forced to participate in the visitation over her mother's objections until she turned eighteen."

"Wow, that's a tough upbringing." And it matched perfectly with what she had told him. Alex let out a sigh of relief. He'd thought she was being honest with him—but his suspicious nature felt better now that he had some corroborating proof.

"The story gets better, though," Tony said. "After high school, she went to Loyola University in Chicago on full scholarship and got an accounting degree, then got her MBA. She was hired immediately at Carver Enterprises, and quickly worked herself up the ladder until she was the senior accountant for Roderick Carver, the CEO. She's one smart cookie." Tony cleared his throat again. "But from the information you sent me, you know what happened after that."

"Like I told you before, she claims that Justin Carver is after her because she saw him kill his father. Do you know if anyone did a thorough investigation into the supposed suicide?"

"No charges have been filed against anyone. From the looks of the reports I've read, the company suffered significant losses right before his death. Unfortunately there isn't a lot of information floating around regarding the details. His son runs the business now, and apparently he's not doing such a terrific job. The company revenues have dropped substantially and the stock price has plummeted."

Alex shook his head. "Amazing. Anything else?"

"Well…" Tony said roughly. "Justin Carver is a force to be reckoned with, that's for sure. Apparently he is a rather nasty individual with a mean streak a mile wide. He's got a record—some ex-girlfriends charged him with assault—but nothing ever went to trial. The charges were always dropped or settled out of court. And there were some other minor charges. But I'd say it's probably only a matter of time before he's linked to some sort of serious criminal activity—whether it turns out to be embezzlement like you suggested or something else more violent is anybody's guess. The media doesn't think much of him, either. I read a few stories that were less than complimentary."

Alex slowly rubbed his chin. "Have you found any proof of the embezzlement yet?"

"Not yet. I'm pretty sure I can hack into his files with a great malware program I've got. I'll send him an email with an offer he can't refuse, and once he opens it, it'll be smooth sailing. Just shoot me an email with what you're looking for and I'll give it a try."

"That's great news, Tony! I knew I could count on you. Chelsea and I will put together an email and send you everything we've discovered so far."

Tony clicked his tongue. "Sure thing, Alex. I'll wait to hear from you."

Alex answered pensively. "You've given me a lot of very valuable information and I appreciate your efforts. Send your bill to my office. I can't thank you enough."

"No problem. And, hey, be careful out there. Carver and his men are dangerous. Watch your back."

"Sure thing." Alex closed his cell phone, set it on the desk and then started pacing. He was glad to have some good news to tell Chelsea, and equally glad to finally know her real name. *Cecilia Eliana Rigo.* It fit her, and he liked the way it sounded as it rolled off of his tongue.

He sat for a moment and ran his hands through his hair, then jumped to his feet again. He needed to talk to Chelsea to let her know about these latest developments. He knocked on the adjoining door that connected his room to Miss Abigail's and entered to find the elderly lady comfortably ensconced in a lounge chair watching a pay-per-view movie, still sipping her soda. Chelsea stood nearby, folding and putting away some clothes that had just been delivered from the hotel cleaners. He greeted both women, then caught Chelsea's eye. "Are you up for a walk on the beach? The sun will be setting soon."

Chelsea raised an eyebrow but before she could answer, Miss Abigail chimed into the conversation. "Oh, yes, please take her out for a walk, Alex. She's been working nonstop since that dreadful episode at the mall today and she definitely needs a break."

"Are you sure it's safe out there?" she asked.

"The hotel posted extra men throughout the building and on the beach for the rest of our stay here, just in case there's a problem," Alex answered. "I spoke with the security chief earlier this afternoon."

Chelsea raised an eyebrow as she finished folding a shirt and put it away in the drawer. "I still haven't finished putting away the laundry…"

Miss Abigail gave Chelsea a wink and shooed her toward the door with her hands. "We've had a traumatic couple of days, my dear. Go take a break for a few minutes. I insist."

Chelsea looked from Alex to Miss Abigail, but finally shrugged and closed the dresser drawer. "Okay. I guess the beach it is." She grabbed her sunglasses and exchanged the new sandals she'd bought at the hotel gift shop for a pair of flip-flops. Alex motioned toward the door and then followed her out, his features thoughtful. Chelsea seemed a bit distant and he wondered if there was more on her mind than just the events from the mall.

As soon as they reached the sand, he turned to her. "Are you feeling okay? You don't seem like yourself."

"I've got a lot on my mind," she admitted, but didn't elaborate.

They reached the edge of the water and Alex looked around, then started heading south since there were hardly any other people in that direction—less likely they'd be overheard. He was pleased to notice a security guard here and there, discreetly observing the area. He kicked at the sand as he walked, wondering where to start.

Finally he reached over and took Chelsea's hand. Her skin was soft and for a moment he just walked, enjoying the contact. He cleared his throat and pressed forward. "First of all, Chelsea, I owe you an apology. I'm really sorry about the way I've been treating you since the beginning of this trip, and I just didn't want to wait any longer before admitting my mistake."

Chelsea stopped walking and bit her bottom lip. "Mistake? What mistake?"

He took a breath and tugged gently on her hand to start her walking again. "Miss Abigail told me before the trip that she was thinking of changing her will and naming you as the executor for her estate. I was immediately suspicious of you and was convinced you were a con artist. I figured you had somehow manipulated her into changing her will, and the entire reason I came to Hawaii was to stop you from tricking her and make sure Miss Abigail was safe. Now that I'm getting to know you better, I realize that you aren't trying to take advantage of her after all. I'm sorry for the way I behaved."

Chelsea took a step back, her eyes widening as the full impact of his words seemed to register. "I didn't know a thing about her will, I promise. This is the first

I'm hearing of it. I don't care about her money. I mean, I'm glad she was able to give me a job, but I would have helped her out regardless."

Alex picked up a shell from the beach and tossed it into the surf. "I realize that now, and I really am sorry for the way I treated you, especially when you were already dealing with so much."

Chelsea walked in silence for a few moments, then put her hand on his arm and squeezed lightly. "No wonder you thought I was a con artist. I probably would have thought the same thing if our positions were reversed. And since you saved my life yesterday, and today, I have to say I'm grateful you're here, even if I am a little hurt by your initial motives."

Alex was quiet for a moment, thankful for her graciousness. Based on her past and history of domestic violence, he knew now that he never should have bullied her, either. At some point, he wanted to make that right, too. He stopped and looked her in the eye but didn't let go of her hand. "I know who you are, Cecilia."

Chelsea's eyes rounded and she started to shake her head and step back. But Alex wouldn't let her go, even though she pulled against his grip.

"Don't go, Cecilia."

"My name is Chelsea," she said softly, her voice cracking.

"Your name is Cecilia Eliana Rigo. You went to Loyola University and you earned a MBA. Sound familiar?"

Chelsea's face paled and she shook her head again. "I need to get back to check on Miss Abigail." She continued to pull her hand away and he finally let go. She turned and headed back up the beach, walking quickly.

Alex followed her closely behind.

"You already told me about Carver. You must have known I'd discover your identity eventually. Why are you so upset?"

"I know it doesn't make sense," Chelsea said, her voice high. "I'm just scared. I went to great lengths to hide myself, and in just a few days you've discovered my entire past. If you can find out my identity that easily, then I'll never be safe." Her breath was coming in gasps and Alex stopped her retreat and pulled her into his arms.

"I'm not going to abandon you just because I know the truth. I'm going to help you. Together, we're going to get through this. Don't forget, we have a plan." His words surprised even him with how deeply he meant them. He wanted to protect her and to keep her safe. He might not be ready for a relationship, as Miss Abigail was hoping, but he could at least help her survive this ordeal until Carver was brought to justice.

"There's been a development—one that will help ease your mind. Tony, my private investigator, is a whiz with computers. He says he thinks he can hack into Justin's system if we send him the search parameters and tell him what we're looking for. He's waiting for us to send him a list."

She nodded, but looked distracted.

"What's wrong?" Alex asked. "I thought you'd be more pleased."

Chelsea wouldn't meet his eyes. "I'm just overwhelmed. A little over a month ago I was leading a normal life in Chicago. My biggest worry was staying on top of Roderick Carver's accounting needs and deciding what to do on a Saturday night. Now I've seen two murders and my life is in danger." She paused, and when she spoke again, he could barely hear her. "I don't know if I can do this. I wouldn't wish this nightmare on anyone."

Alex touched Chelsea's chin, then gently raised her head so that he could see her eyes. They were wide and troubled. "With God's help, you can, Cecilia. Miss Abigail just told me tonight that I needed more God in my life and she was right. Maybe we both can learn from her and put this entire situation in God's hands." His eyes locked with hers.

"After everything that has happened, I'd imagine your instincts are probably telling you to run. But you're doing the right thing by staying and fighting off the fear. Miss Abigail needs you to be in Maui the day after tomorrow when she goes to the hospital. It could make the difference between life and death for her." He paused and brushed some hair out of her face. "Mr. Westin will be here tonight, and hotel security is on the alert. Tomorrow we'll leave early in the morning and spend the day on one of the other islands as an extra precaution to make sure you're safe. You're going to make it through this, and I'm going to do everything I can to help you."

TEN

Chelsea rubbed her forehead, trying to sort out her next move. She had barely slept at all during the night, and this morning's early flight to Oahu, one of the nearby islands, hadn't helped. The one-hour flight hadn't been too bouncy, but since her nerves were already raw, the short trip had awakened her fear of flying yet again, adding another level of stress to her already anxiety-riddled life. She was convinced that she had made a huge mistake by promising Alex to stay until the surgery date. It was just too dangerous—even if they had escaped to Oahu for the day.

Yet for the first time that she could remember, she had someone in her life to share her burdens. The question now was whether or not she should let herself depend on him. She stole a look at Alex, who was sorting through the tickets they had just purchased for the snorkeling trip. He sure was an attractive man, and his dark hair and strong jaw made tingles dance across her skin. He had proved himself to be a man of his word and had protected her from the Braves fan at the mall. He even knew part of her history and had still refused to abandon her. *But could she trust him?* So many men had let her down in her life. It seemed almost impossible to risk being hurt by yet another one. Her heart pounded so hard that it seemed it would break right out of her chest as another wave of fear and indecision swept over her.

Despite Alex's promises, she still wanted to run. Justin Carver was aware of her location, and even though the man with the Braves cap was in jail, it was only a matter of time before Justin sent another henchman her way. She hugged herself, putting her hands under her arms to stop them from shaking. It didn't seem to help.

She tried to consider her options, but she really didn't have any. She didn't want to put Abigail and Alex in danger any longer. Was there a way to disappear but still stay close for the surgery, just in case? She could never forgive herself if Miss Abigail had life-threatening complications and she hadn't been available for a transfusion. And how could she prove Carver's guilt without Alex's help? He was the one that had found the computer expert they could use to bring Carver down. But what if one of them was killed by Carver in his quest to silence her? She felt utterly trapped. What should she do?

She chewed her bottom lip in frustration. She had never felt so alone and lost in her entire life. Her life before Roderick Carver's murder seemed like a distant memory. On shaky legs, she stood and walked over to where Miss Abigail and Alex were waiting to board the boat that was going to take them on the half-day snorkeling trip.

Suddenly, Miss Abigail touched her abdomen and

grimaced. "I'm sorry to say that this boat trip might not be a good idea for me, after all."

Chelsea quickly took her arm and led her over to a set of chairs under a dark blue awning. "Is your stomach bothering you?"

Miss Abigail adjusted her hat. "Hmm. Yes, I'm sorry, my dear. I think I might just better sit this one out."

Alex put his hands on his hips, a look of concern on his face. "Is there anything we can do? Do we need to call an ambulance?"

Miss Abigail waved away his question. "No, no. It's just more of the same Crohn's disease symptoms I've been battling for a while now. Thankfully, the surgery tomorrow will take care of all of this. I just don't think I can handle being on a boat that's swaying back and forth. It would be a bit much."

"That's okay, Miss Abigail. We'll get you back over to Maui as soon as we can and let you rest. Perhaps this entire day was a bit ambitious," Chelsea said as she took out her cell phone. "I'll call the airlines right now and have our tickets changed."

Miss Abigail shook her head. "Oh, no. I still want you and Alex to go. I'll just find a cool spot to sit with Mr. Westin and take it easy while I wait for your return."

"We don't need to go if you're not going," Alex said.

"Yes, you do, Alex." Miss Abigail confirmed. "You and Chelsea have been stressed to the limit by the past few days. I don't know why all of this has been happening, but I do know that I want you to have at least a couple of hours of relaxation."

"But…" Chelsea protested.

Miss Abigail's face took on an air of unwavering determination. "But nothing," she said firmly. "Look, I can wait right here just fine, and if Mr. Westin doesn't mind, he can wait here with me. There are a couple of little shops right across the street, so if I start feeling better, he can escort me while I do a bit of shopping. Consider the trip my present to the both of you. It's the least I can do for dragging you both across the United States on my account."

Chelsea considered the situation carefully. If Mr. Westin stayed with Miss Abigail, then the elderly matron would certainly be safe. It was also doubtful Carver would attempt to kidnap Chelsea from a boat filled with people, especially with Alex by her side—presuming he even knew where to find her at the moment. They were on Oahu, a totally different island from Maui, and hadn't seen any sign of Carver or his minions during their trip. They hadn't actually bought their tickets this morning until they had arrived at the airport, and they had tried to cover their tracks. The circumstances seemed safe enough, and she desperately wanted to feel normal again, even if it was for just a few short hours.

Chelsea looked at Alex and was surprised to see genuine pleasure in his expression. Was he truly looking forward to spending time with her on the boat? The idea amazed her, but at the same time sent a warm shimmer through her middle. She looked into his gray eyes and a whisper of attraction swept over her. Could she really push aside her fear and relax with Alex for a few hours of snorkeling on the reef?

She regarded Mr. Westin from head to toe. She had

to admit that he looked perfectly capable of keeping Miss Abigail safe.

She glanced back at Alex, who nodded at her and held his hand out. She found herself yearning for a chance to spend some time with him without fear dogging her every step. The more she knew him, the more she liked. Yes, he was a workaholic and rough around the edges, but he was also caring and considerate, and as she gazed into his eyes, she felt another level of trust growing inside her. He'd said he would protect her. His smile also melted her heart like a Popsicle in the hot summer sun.

A few people started to board and Chelsea glanced over at the boat. "I don't know if this is a good idea or not," she murmured to herself.

Alex was close enough to hear her and took a step closer. "Why not?"

"Because I don't have time for snorkeling. I really need to just pack up and go. I've already put you in enough danger."

"Chelsea," Alex said, his voice low as he touched her in the small of the back and gently nudged her toward the boat. "I know you have a lot on your mind, but please, let's just take a day to recover from everything that has happened. The world and all its troubles will still be waiting when we finish the trip, but you'll have some great photos to add to your scrapbook."

Chelsea gave him a tentative smile and bit her bottom lip, unsure.

Alex grabbed her hand. "Look, we're a long way from Maui and nobody even knows you're here besides the four of us. Miss Abigail is safe. You're safe. I'll be with you the entire time, I promise. And you promised me you'd stay until the surgery, remember?" His eyes were intense and filled with hope.

She squeezed his hand. Alex's attention made her feel good about herself and gave her a confidence she hadn't felt in a long time. Wise or not, Chelsea wanted to trust him a bit more and to steal this last day of happiness before her life was upended and she was forced to disappear into anonymity once again.

Chelsea's eyes locked with his, drawn in by the caring and warmth in their depths. "You win, Alex. Let's go see the reef." She was packed and ready to go once they returned to Maui and Miss Abigail arrived in the recovery room at the hospital, but for today, her last day in paradise, she would enjoy herself and pretend Justin Carver didn't exist. It was probably the last time she would ever get that luxury, so she grabbed hold with both hands and stepped out on the fragile ledge of trust.

ELEVEN

The water lapped quietly against the sides of the boat as it bobbed in the gentle waves. It was a perfect day for taking a dip in the ocean. The wind was nonexistent and the sky was cloudless and clear. Chelsea put on her fins and mask, then jumped into the water and started swimming. After a short distance she turned to look for Alex. He was about twenty feet away and gave her a thumbs-up sign right before he put on his mask to dive below the surface.

The water was like liquid crystal. She could see all the way to the bottom of the reef, a distance the guide had told them was about thirty feet. They were anchored in a small cove where the sea turtles were known to frequent, and she had already seen several after only a short time in the water, not to mention a host of beautiful tropical fish. The locals had dubbed the area Turtle Town, and the site was now a must-see on most snorkeling excursions. Even now there were two other boats anchored nearby, each hosting at least forty passengers who were jumping in and out of the water to enjoy the view.

Chelsea swam a little farther and snapped some

more photos. She was pleased she had stopped at the dive shop by the pier to buy a special digital camera for taking pictures underwater. So far she had taken more than a hundred shots of the coral reef and the varied marine life. She took another shot and then turned off the camera, letting it dangle from the rubber wrist strap. The current was strong and she had to concentrate on her swimming to stay clear of the lava rocks that jutted out from below. She hadn't meant to get so far away from the boat, but when she was taking pictures, it was hard not to swim just a little farther for that one special shot. She wasn't sure where Alex had gone but she knew he was staying close. She glanced around, looking for his snorkel poking through the waves.

The first tug on her leg felt as though she had snagged her fin against a rock. But the second tug was more forceful and she struggled to pull free. When she looked down, she discovered that it was no rock that held her fin, but rather a strong male hand that quickly moved to her ankle.

Her heart started beating frantically and she struggled even harder. She couldn't make out many of his features because they were distorted by the diving mask and the air regulator, but the diver's hair was lighter and longer than Alex's, and he seemed like a very big man. A tremor of fear shot down her spine as the man's grip grew even tighter and he started to pull her toward the shore. Her head went under repeatedly and she clawed for the surface as the panic overcame her. Her breath came in gasps and within a few seconds she couldn't breathe at all as her snorkel filled with water. She thrashed about, trying to free herself, but couldn't escape from the punishing grip the man had on her ankle.

And this far from the surface, she couldn't even scream.

Alex pulled himself up on the boat and turned to sit on the diving platform, his legs and fins still dangling in the water. He couldn't have asked for a more beautiful place to swim. He hoped Chelsea was enjoying the trip as much as he was. He scanned the water in the vicinity where he had seen her a few minutes before, looking for signs of her snorkel. At first he saw nothing, but then he saw someone struggling and flailing in the water and his heart gripped in fear. Chelsea was drowning!

His adrenaline surged and he dove back into the water, swimming as fast as he possibly could to help her before it was too late.

He arrived quickly on the scene and saw what was really going on: there was a man beneath her who was pulling on her ankle. He grabbed the man's neck from behind and pulled at the regulator on his scuba gear, but didn't quite get it out of his adversary's mouth. Bubbles swirled around both of them in a mad dance to the surface as the men wrestled for control. The attacker's head twisted but he punched out at Alex and managed to strike him hard near his ear, causing Alex to fall away from him.

He bounced to the surface and grabbed a great gulp of air, then dove down and went after the regulator again, this time managing to wrench it away from the man's mouth in another wave of bubbles. He pushed down hard on the man's air tank, throwing the assailant off balance, then pushed him away from Chelsea with such force that the man lost his grip on Chelsea's ankle.

Alex could tell that his adversary was strong, but Alex was the better swimmer. And as determined as the man was to drag Chelsea away, Alex was even more determined not to let it happen. The man kicked frantically and grabbed for his regulator but before he could clench it Alex punched him hard in the stomach and kicked him even farther away from Chelsea. The attacker recovered from the blows and reached for his regulator again. Somehow he managed to get it back into his mouth just as Alex returned from grabbing another breath of air at the surface. With a swoosh, the assailant retreated, leaving a trail of bubbles behind him as he swam away.

Alex grasped Chelsea's arm and pulled her quickly to the surface, keeping an eye out for the attacker in case he decided to return. A few seconds later Alex caught sight of him swimming toward the shore near a row of volcanic rock. Alex was tempted to chase after him, but knew that his first priority had to be getting Chelsea safely back to the boat.

His head broke through the water and he immediately sucked in a breath and turned his attention to Chelsea. She was still conscious, thankfully, but she was clearly in a state of panic. Her arms were flailing and she was trying frantically to suck in huge gulps of air but was taking in a large amount of water, as well. Alex tried to help her but she turned, frantically lashing out at him, obviously not recognizing him or his desire to help.

He grabbed both of her wrists and quickly twisted her around so that her back was against his chest. The rush of adrenaline and fear had made her strong and it was all he could do just to hold her. She was in full panic mode and fought him with every bit of strength she had. She was gasping for air and completely out of control.

"Chelsea! It's me! It's Alex. Listen to my voice, okay? Stop fighting me and hold still. I'm trying to help you. You're safe now. I'm going to take you to the boat." He immobilized her as best as he could to keep her from hurting either one of them and simply treaded water for a few moments until her energy was spent. He continued speaking to her in soft tones the entire time.

Finally her body relaxed somewhat and she lay limp in his arms, though her breathing was still ragged and gurgling. Alex loosened his grip slightly, then swam back to the boat with her, his strong legs slicing through the water. He continued to scan the area as he swam, but saw no further sign of the attacker. He wasn't even sure he would recognize the assailant if he saw him again. His view had been distorted by the water, the fighting and the scuba gear the man had been wearing. But he kept his eyes open anyway, looking for any signs of danger.

"Easy, Chelsea. It's me, Alex. You're safe now. No one's going to hurt you." He continued to murmur to her in soothing tones as he swam, at the same time condemning himself for putting her in danger. He shouldn't have made her come on this boat trip. He should have found somewhere secure for her to stay, somewhere Carver's men couldn't find her.

By the time they reached the boat, her body was racked with choking and trembling. He could tell that her brain seemed foggy and she was fighting to stay in the here and now as she coughed up water and mucus, shivering violently all the while.

The guide from the boat had seen them coming and rushed to help Alex get Chelsea on board. Together they pulled her limp body up to the deck as she continued to choke and take in great gulps of air. They lay her on her stomach on the deck of the boat and extended her arms so the water could drain out of her mouth. Her face was pale and her lips had turned a dark bluish color. Several of the other passengers rushed over to help and handed him towels to wrap around her, but there was really nothing else that could be done aside from waiting for Chelsea to regain her strength.

Alex motioned everyone back, trying to give her some space. CPR wasn't necessary since she was breathing on her own, but she was disoriented and scared and he didn't want a crowd frightening her even more than she was already. Water streamed out of her mouth and nose as she sputtered and gagged. Finally she succumbed to the blackness and just lay still, unconscious.

Alex sat by her side and gently pulled her head and shoulders into his lap so he could keep an eye on her breathing. He carefully brushed the hair out of her eyes and was glad to see some of the color coming back into her lips and cheeks. Silently he thanked God for letting him see her distress in time to save her. He sat back and leaned against the side of the boat, his mind whirling as he felt the boat engines start up and head for the docks. It had to have been God that prompted him to look for her at just the right time. There was no other explanation. He silently wondered if he'd been missing God's promptings in other areas of his life for the past few years.

Miss Abigail had been right. In the aftermath of Irene's betrayal, he had just wanted to shut himself off from the pain and humiliation he'd felt, so he'd turned all of his attention to his work. He had focused so much on building his career that he had put everything else on a back burner, including his relationship with God. It had been a mistake. With a thankful heart, he closed his eyes and prayed for forgiveness.

When he opened his eyes a few moments later, he looked at Chelsea, who was still motionless in his arms. He felt his heart squeeze. He had experienced true fear when he had seen the attacker pulling Chelsea under, and had known at that very moment that what he was feeling for her went beyond friendship. But was he truly ready for another lady in his life? Was it worth living through all the pain again if he was wrong about her or if they couldn't make it work? After all, he'd only know Chelsea for a few days, and his breakup with Irene had made him feel as if someone had taken out his heart and stomped on it.

He gently stroked Chelsea's hair. Was God giving him a second chance with Chelsea? He touched her cheek and traced his finger along her jaw. She was a beautiful woman, both inside and out. Why hadn't he seen it before? He had wasted so much time being suspicious of her, and now he knew instinctively that their remaining time together would be short. With this new proof that she was putting him in danger with her presence, he was certain she would try to leave him the moment she regained her strength.

Lord, please look out for this amazing lady. Help her recover, and help her trust me so that we can face this danger together. Amen.

TWELVE

Chelsea awoke with a groan and glanced around the hospital room. Bits and pieces of the day gradually returned to her memory. She vaguely remembered the trip to the hospital and the doctors drawing blood and taking a chest x-ray. There was a monitor on her finger testing for oxygenation, and she felt tubes in her nose that were delivering oxygen to her, as well.

But despite the physical evidence, the whole thing seemed like one incredibly nasty nightmare. She moaned and rubbed her head, trying to ease the horrible ache behind her eyes. Once again, someone had tried to abduct her—and this time they had very nearly succeeded in drowning her in the process. Only a few more moments beneath the water and she knew instinctively that she wouldn't have made it.

She looked around the small room and saw Alex sitting in a chair that was obviously too small for him. He had moved the chair so that he was blocking the door. His eyes were closed and he appeared to be sleeping fitfully. She wondered fleetingly if Miss Abigail had made it safely back to the hotel in Maui with Mr. Westin, and a wave of guilty trepidation assailed her.

She had been foolish to think she could have a day's escape from danger. Quite clearly, danger would follow her wherever she went—and it would put those around her at risk.

The thought of Miss Abigail and Alex in peril made her heart constrict as a wave of sadness overwhelmed her. She was also terrified of losing her life to Carver and the terror that he undoubtedly had planned for her. He was extremely determined to get her in his clutches, as evidenced by these multiple kidnapping attempts.

Pain and anger warred for supremacy in her tangled emotions. She took a deep breath, her chest heavy with effort. She was tired of constantly looking over her shoulder and already apprehensive about the loneliness that would undoubtedly consume her future. Would it never end?

Alex stirred and shifted, then noticed that Chelsea was also awake. He gifted her with one of his rare smiles. "Well, I'm glad you're back among the living. That was a pretty close call." He stood and stretched, then moved to her bedside, his gaze intense.

"How is Miss Abigail?" Chelsea asked quietly, her voice hoarse.

"She's doing well. Mr. Westin got her safely back to Maui and is being extra vigilant after what happened to you at the beach. Thankfully, she's still planning on going through with the surgery tomorrow. I got a call from the doctor while you were sleeping and he again expressed that it was imperative that you were near the hospital during the operation. He actually wanted you in the surgical waiting room, but I told him that was impossible. We agreed that near the hospital would have to be good enough."

Alex studied Chelsea carefully and felt a wave of relief wash over him. She was clearly exhausted, but according to the doctor she would survive her close encounter in the water with no ill effects. A surge of protectiveness resurfaced. He reached over and gently held Chelsea's hand. "How are you feeling?"

She sighed and swallowed. "My chest hurts, but I guess overall I'm just happy to be alive." Her voice was rough and he could tell that her throat was also hurting when she spoke.

He gripped her hand a little tighter. "I'd thought I'd lost you." His gray eyes narrowed and held hers with a fierce intensity.

A doctor entered the room and Alex reluctantly released Chelsea's hand and backed up while she talked to the patient. They had been in this emergency room for more than six hours and, hopefully, Chelsea was about to be released. The doctor listened to her lungs once again, then declared Chelsea fit enough to leave as long as she got plenty of rest, stayed away from the beaches for a while and returned for a follow-up visit in three days.

After the doctor left, Chelsea sat up slowly and swallowed hard. "I can't go back to the hotel. It will put both you and Miss Abigail in too much danger. Carver is bound to have somebody there waiting for me to arrive. It's just too dangerous." Tears filled her eyes. "How is she going to manage without my help? And what about the surgery tomorrow? She could die if they have a problem and they don't have enough blood to help her, but how can I even go back to Maui?"

"We'll work out something," Alex said softly as he touched her shoulder. "I've been making plans for the past couple of hours and have gotten some of the bases covered. Mr. Westin will help make sure Miss Abigail stays safe for now, and we can work out the rest as we go. I'm waiting to hear back from a church in Maui. I think the pastor might be able to help."

He could see the panic in her eyes and could tell her mind was working a mile a minute. Was she even listening to him? "Chelsea, you're not alone on this. I'm going to help you. Do you hear me? I know this is a lot to hit you all at once but we can work through it. Talk to me. What are you thinking?"

She wrapped her arms around herself and closed her eyes for a moment. "My mind seems like a jumbled mess right now and I've got quite a headache." She rubbed her forehead. "I guess the first thing I need is to find a place to hide and a way for the hospital to contact me if I'm needed tomorrow. Then once the surgery is over, I have to get back to the mainland immediately and disappear before Carver finds me." Chelsea glanced up at the clock. "Right now I have to get out of here before Carver realizes I'm not dead. How long have I been here?"

"A few hours."

"Then it's already too late. He probably has somebody out in the lobby watching the exits. Maybe more than one person." The enormity of the situation seemed to hit her all at once and more tears trickled down her cheeks. "How will I ever know who to trust again? How will I ever be safe?"

Alex pulled her into a gentle embrace. "We're going to figure something out. I promise."

A few moments passed as she rested her head on his shoulder and leaned into his strength. She seemed to fit perfectly in his arms and Alex softly rubbed her back, hoping to sooth her fears and encourage her to trust him.

Finally she lifted her head. "Did the police come by?"

"They came and went. I'm supposed to take you over to the station once you've been released from the hospital. You'll have to tell them exactly what happened once we get over there."

She glanced around the room and slowly pulled away from him. "You can't take me to the police station. I'll get there on my own somehow. You've got to get as far away from me as possible."

"I can't leave you alone—"

"Yes, you can, and you will!" Her voice was sharp but she softened it and touched his cheek where it had been bruised by the latest encounter. "Don't you see? You're in danger just by being in the same room with me."

Alex was silent for a moment, considering his response. "You might be right. That man at the mall would have probably killed me if that guard hadn't showed up, and the man at the beach didn't hesitate to hurt me, either. But knowing that doesn't scare me off. I want to stay and help you, and that's exactly what I'm going to do. It's my choice."

More tears started flowing down her cheeks and Alex went instantly to her side and pulled her into another warm embrace. "It's okay, Chelsea. This problem is Carver's making, not yours."

"I'm just so scared. I should have left after I got that

note, but I kept hoping I could find some evidence to take to the police. I was living in a fantasy world." She exhaled. "Maybe going back to Maui now is a big mistake, as well. Maybe Miss Abigail should reschedule her surgery until we can find someone else that can help her."

"She can't do that. I asked the doctor about postponing it when he called earlier, but he said she really needs the surgery done tomorrow. Her Crohn's disease has reached a critical stage. That's why she was in pain this morning." Alex could see her withdrawing, considering options, and not keeping him in the equation. It was written all over her face.

"Look. Let's get things straight right here and now. I'm not leaving, and you're not going through this alone. I'm going to stay and help you. I'll make sure Miss Abigail gets to her surgery and that she gets back home to Tallahassee safely, too. That's a promise, by the way. Something I don't make lightly.

"In the meantime, I'm going to make sure you're also safe, and that means starting by getting you to the police station." He held up a hand to cut off her protests. "I know you're not willing to tell them everything, but you need to let them know enough to keep you safe. And along those lines, I also have a brother who is a U.S. Marshal. I'll be giving him a call, as well. I don't know how all of this is going to turn out, Chelsea, but I do know I'm not going to abandon you."

She leaned against the bed for support, her body trembling. Alex noticed and gently cupped her face and brought her around to look at him. He placed a light kiss on her forehead. "You're not alone. Let me help you. Trust me, Cecilia. Please." Alex could see the battle in her eyes, but there was no way he was going to abandon her now. Whether she wanted his help or not, he was going to give it. Somehow they were going to make it through this, but as far as he was concerned, they were going to do it together.

THIRTEEN

"And did you get a good look at this person who was trying to drag you under the water?" The policeman didn't even look up when he asked the question; he just kept filling out his form. The man was obviously going through the motions and Alex's patience was starting to wear pretty thin.

"No, of course not. He was covered in scuba gear. Besides, it all happened so fast and I was trying to stay alive." Chelsea looked at Alex and rolled her eyes. "Look, I don't mean to be rude, but is there somebody else we should talk to? You obviously don't believe me."

That comment finally made the man look up. He regarded Chelsea in silence for a moment, then put down his pen. "It's not a question of believing or not believing, ma'am. You're giving me very little to go on, and without proof, there's not much I can investigate. I understand that you had some trouble over on Maui, but that gentleman is in jail, and obviously didn't try to abduct you on the beach this morning. That case is closed." He leaned back in his chair. "I'm hoping the more questions I ask, the more you'll tell me and the more I'll have to actually build a case against this unknown attacker."

Chelsea stiffened her spine. "Well, I didn't realize I had to make your case for you. I thought since I was the target here and obviously in danger that you might want to actually investigate and gather evidence. Do they really pay you to sit there and antagonize the victims?"

Alex gently put his hand on her shoulder. "Easy now." He turned to the policeman who had noticed his hand and had raised an eyebrow. "Listen, Officer… Metcalf, was it? I'm sure you understand that this situation has been very stressful. We came here straight from the hospital, and all we're asking is that you check into this and give Ms. Rogers some protection."

"I'd like to help you, but you have to understand that I just don't have any extra men to assign to a protection detail right now. Look, it's not uncommon for a victim to be scared after a stalking incident and to think that others are also out to get her."

Chelsea narrowed her eyes. "Thanks so much for your help." She spun around on her heel and walked as quickly as she could back into the foyer of the building, her jaw set. Alex was close behind her and he grabbed her arm as she was about to push through the front doors. There were a few people milling around so he pulled her into a nearby hallway entrance out of sight so they could talk in private.

"Hey! Wait a minute."

"See why I don't like policemen?" She was fuming. "They're all the same. That's exactly how they used to react when I told them about my father's abuse. They always believed his word over mine."

"Where do you think you're going?"

"Back to Maui and then... I don't know. I have to hole up somewhere. Fast."

"Okay, I'll call a cab."

Chelsea shook her head. "Carver's men will probably have the cabbies covered. Alex, please just go. I've got to do this disappearing act by myself. I don't want you in the line of fire any longer. I appreciate all you've done, but now it's time for me to go it alone." A part of her wanted to lean on him and accept his help, but she still wasn't ready to depend upon someone else for her survival. No, she could only depend upon herself. This latest fiasco with the police was just further proof of that. Every man in her life had disappointed her, and even though Alex had helped her quite a bit in the past couple of days, she didn't want to depend upon him completely. It was too much, too soon. She just couldn't do it.

Alex's lips thinned into an expression of grim determination. "I'm sticking with you, Chelsea. Haven't you heard one word I've said all afternoon? Not all men are going to let you down. I'm not going to leave you to face this on your own. Please give me just a little bit of trust and let me show you."

She didn't reply—but she didn't walk away. Alex chose to view that as agreement and went back into planning mode. "You're probably right about the cab. The first thing we need is a ready supply of cash. After that, we need alternate transportation." He opened his wallet and found that he only had about a hundred dollars with him. It wasn't much, but it was a start. "Let's find a back way out of this place." He reached for her hand and gently started to lead her into the foyer but then stopped. Out of the corner of his eye, he noticed there was a new man standing at the counter in front of Officer Metcalf's desk. If he listened carefully, he could just make out part of the conversation. He pulled Chelsea close against the wall so they were both completely out of sight and motioned for her to stay quiet.

"Yeah, I'm looking for my sister. She's about five foot six with brown eyes and long brown hair. Real pretty, nice smile. Anyway, she had some kind of swimming accident at the beach this morning, and she said she was going to come over here and report it to the police. She probably had her boyfriend with her—a big guy about six foot three wearing a white T-shirt with a fish logo on the pocket. Have you seen them? I was supposed to meet them here, but I can't seem to find them."

Alex snuck a quick look around the corner and saw Officer Metcalf motioning with his hand toward the paperwork on his desk. The man he was talking to had short brown hair and was wearing khaki pants and a red-collared shirt. Alex couldn't see his face from the angle where they were hidden, but he was the right height to be the man who'd attacked them earlier. He seemed rather muscular and held himself like an impatient man on a mission.

"Yeah, they were in here a few minutes ago," Officer Metcalf replied. "She's a real pistol, that sister of yours. She claimed a man tried to drown her on the beach."

The man in the red shirt laughed. "Yeah, she has an active imagination. Did you happen to see which direction they went when they left? Maybe I can still catch them."

The officer pointed toward the front door. "Through

there, I think. I honestly wasn't paying that close attention."

The man made a point of reading the policeman's name tag. "Thanks, Officer Metcalf. I appreciate your help. Hopefully, I can still catch up with them."

The officer returned to his paperwork and the man turned and headed back out the front door, glancing around the foyer as he did so. Thankfully, Alex and Chelsea were still out of his line of sight, but Alex shrank back even farther, just in case. He still couldn't get a look at the man's face, but he watched him exit the building and disappear into the parking lot.

Alex waited a few more minutes to make sure the man didn't return, then turned to Chelsea and started leading her down the hallway in the opposite direction. They abandoned the police station and entered the surrounding neighborhood on foot, walking quickly through yards and staying off the sidewalks. A few blocks later they came upon a long strip mall with two large department stores and a slew of other businesses. Alex looked behind them several times as they made their way into the clothing store but didn't see anyone suspicious. He hoped that leaving on foot and staying on the move would throw anyone following them off track, at least long enough for them to make some changes in their appearances.

He gave Chelsea fifty dollars and nodded toward the clothes racks. "Try to find a new shirt that's a different color than the one you have on now. I'll meet you at the front of the store in ten minutes. Then we'll see about getting some more cash."

"Deal," she said quickly. She reached for his hand

and gave it a squeeze, then turned and quickly disappeared among the other customers.

Alex watched her go, a knot forming in the pit of his stomach. Would she be back, or would she try to go it on her own?

Lord, please help her come back to me. Help her learn to trust me, and help me to keep her safe.

A few minutes later Chelsea met Alex at the front of the store as promised, and Alex gave a sigh of relief. So far she was playing along with his plans. He hoped that her actions showed she was slowly starting to trust him. They donned their new clothes and crossed the street to a local bank. Alex withdrew a large sum of money and split it with Chelsea so they'd each have some cash readily available in case they got separated. It was a risk to give her the means to go it alone, but he figured he couldn't expect her to trust him without giving her some trust in the first place. They took a few minutes to hatch a plan in a corner of the bank lobby, then exited separately and walked over to the nearby strip mall.

Alex went straight to the drug store and bought a few necessities while Chelsea went into the beachwear store and bought them both some more new clothes that would help them blend in better with the tourists. Then after making their purchases, they took separate cabs to a cheap hotel in Honolulu they had discovered in the phone book.

When Chelsea knocked on the door at the hotel, Alex gave a sigh of relief, then had to do a double take at her appearance. Instead of the conservative outfits that she had worn while working for Miss Abigail, she was now dressed as a surfer girl, with a flowery sarong and flip-flops. She had also trimmed her hair to shoulder length and streaked it with blond highlights. Carver's men had undoubtedly seen photos of her, but maybe the new look would give them an edge. With her dark skin and new clothes, she looked as if she had just come from the beach. It was quite a change, but she looked amazing, despite how tired she was, and Alex felt a surge of attraction flow through him. Had she always been this beautiful?

"Wow, I hardly recognized you," he said once she was safely inside the room.

Chelsea raised an eyebrow. "Is that a good thing or a bad thing?"

"It's a wonderful thing. You looked great before, but I really like this new look, too." He grabbed her hands and twirled her around until she begged him to stop among peals of laughter. Soon they were both laughing. Alex caught her in his arms and came to a stop. A bolt of electricity seemed to flow between them and they suddenly broke apart.

"I like your laugh. It's really good to hear it," Alex said softly.

Chelsea took a few steps back and sat on one of the chairs. She gave him a tender smile. "There hasn't been a lot to laugh about lately."

"Do you think anyone followed you?"

"I don't know. I didn't see anyone, but that doesn't mean a whole lot." She pulled the clothes and other items she had bought out of her shopping bag and separated them into two blue duffel bags, one for him and one for her.

"Do you think you'll be able to make it without wearing a suit and tie?" she teased.

"It'll be a challenge," he said with a smile.

Alex sorted through his own purchases and helped her pack. Then he sat across from her and picked up a pad. He studied his notes for a moment before meeting Chelsea's eyes once again. "I found a local church that is willing to give Miss Abigail some help over the next few days. They sent a young couple over to stay with her at the hotel and to help her get packed up. Then tomorrow they'll take her to the hospital and stay with her through the surgery. After the surgery, the wife is going to fly back to Tallahassee with her. Once she gets back to town, my brother Ryan is going to send a temporary assistant to stay with her until we get your situation figured out." He flipped a page. "Of course, Mr. Westin will stay with her the entire time she is in Hawaii to ensure her safety as well, but I wanted to make sure she had someone with her that would really give her the care and attention she needs through the surgery and the aftermath."

"That's perfect. Thank you so much." She took a sip from the can of soda he offered her. "What if they need my blood during the operation?"

Alex nodded. "I've taken care of that, too. The head of the surgery department has my cell phone number and was given strict instructions not to give it out to anyone else. If Miss Abigail has any issues, including needing a blood transfusion during the surgery, they will call me immediately." He grabbed another pharmacy bag from the desk and handed it to her. "This is a pay-as-you-go cell phone. I want you to keep it with you at all times so we can communicate if we get separated."

Chelsea nodded and opened the box. It was a pretty

fancy model and boasted texting, internet and an internal GPS. She handed it to Alex who turned it on and started programming it as she flipped through the owner's manual. A few minutes later he handed it back to her.

"Okay, I've programmed my number into your speed dial directory. See here?" He showed her how to find his number and a few other basics about the phone. "Now you know you'll be able to reach me if we get separated. All you have to do is call and I'll come running."

Chelsea's eyes softened. "I'm so glad you got that all worked out. I've been so worried about Miss Abigail and how she was going to make it through all of this alone. You've really helped to put my mind at ease. Do you think she understands the situation?"

"I called Miss Abigail myself before I came to the hotel. I explained as much as I could to her and she's worried about you, but she's fine with our plans."

Chelsea sighed, a look of relief on her face. "What *are* our plans?"

Alex flipped the page on his notebook. "Well, I called my brother Dominic back in Florida. He's the U.S. Marshal I told you about." He paused. "According to his boss, he's on a stakeout or something. Anyway, he's unavailable for the next few hours, so I figured we could hole up here until I hear from him and then we can decide our next move once I hear from him. I'm sure he'll have some good advice." He stood and walked to her side, then gently pulled her into an embrace. Despite his decisions about relationships, he couldn't seem to stop touching her. Maybe he needed to rethink those decisions. She laid her head on his shoulder and for a moment he just enjoyed the closeness.

Finally he spoke. "My next goal is to figure out how to get us back to Maui without being seen. I know you're tired, and today has been one very long, horrible day for you. I rented two rooms here, and yours is just through that door. Why don't you go get some sleep for a couple of hours and I'll keep working on our plans, okay?" He squeezed her hand, then released her as she moved to go through the door.

"You'll wake me up as soon as you have a plan?" she asked.

"Sure." He took a step in her direction. "Will you promise me something?"

Chelsea's eyes widened. "Like what?"

"How about that you won't disappear without me." He took another step. "Look, I know you're worried and scared, and I want you to have your own hotel room so you can have some privacy. But I can't keep working on this with my brother if I also have to be worried that you're going to run when I'm not looking. I need you to trust me, and I want to be able to trust you."

Chelsea seemed to consider his words, and for a moment she just stood there. She took so long to respond that a sliver of fear started to spread across Alex's chest. Was she going to run and try to do this on her own the minute he turned his back?

"Okay," she finally whispered. "I promise to stay with you until we get back to Maui. No running."

Alex raised an eyebrow. He'd hoped for more, but apparently that small promise was all she was willing to give. "Thank you. Everything will work out. You'll see."

Her expression was doubtful, but she gave him a small smile, then turned and disappeared into her room.

Alex went back over to his bed and lay down, his thoughts spinning in his head. What would happen when they got back to Maui? What would he do if she tried to run without him? He knew she was concerned about Miss Abigail, but he had a very bad feeling that as soon as the elderly lady was done with her surgery, Chelsea Rogers would disappear and be out of his life forever.

Alex closed his eyes. He couldn't let that happen. He hadn't had time to really analyze his feelings for Chelsea, but he knew he wasn't ready to lose her.

FOURTEEN

Alex knocked softly on Chelsea's door, then smiled when she came through. "Sorry you only got a few minutes to rest, but we have to go." He turned and put the rest of the items they had purchased in her duffel, then handed it to her. "I found us a boat to Maui, but it leaves in about half an hour, and it's going to take us that long to get to the pier. We have to leave now."

Chelsea nodded and took the bag, glad that she'd at least gotten a chance to close her eyes for a few minutes. The problem was she kept seeing the man attacking her underwater in her mind's eye, so sleep had eluded her. She grabbed her purse and followed Alex out the door and down the hallway, then actually walked into Alex as he stopped short in front of her. He took her hand and pulled her toward an alcove with the hotel's vending machines. He led her to a soda machine and stood protectively in front of her as he looked around the area.

"What's going on?" she whispered.

"I have a taxi waiting downstairs, but there's a man talking to the maid just a few feet away from the car, and he doesn't look like a regular hotel guest—he seems more the bodyguard type. He might even be the guy from the police station, too, but I can't be sure. He could be perfectly harmless, but that's too much coincidence for me."

Chelsea's heartbeat doubled in speed. "What are we going to do?"

Alex paused a moment, then squeezed her hand. "We'll take the back stairs and call for a different taxi a few blocks away. I'd rather be safe than sorry." He glanced at his watch. "Come on, we have to hurry."

He quickly led her away. Within moments they were sprinting from the hotel and darting behind the trees of the nearby lots. About two blocks away, they dropped down behind a group of hydrangea bushes that covered the corner of the property. The thick foliage gave them an excellent hiding place as they crouched behind the blue and purple blossoms.

They caught their breath and then moved so that they had an excellent view of the street. Suddenly, Chelsea grabbed Alex's arm. The man from the hotel was driving a gray sedan slowly down the street. It was obvious that he was looking for them. Chelsea started shaking.

"I can't do this. He's going to kill me. I just know it…"

Alex gently touched Chelsea's chin and turned her head away from the man and the car. "Look at me, Chelsea." She locked her eyes with his and saw the strength and determination there. "I'm going to help you. We're going to make it through this. Together. Keep saying that in your head every time you start worrying. Trust me. Okay?"

She swallowed, still terrified, but a measure of her

fear ebbed at the thought of having Alex by her side. She was so used to handling her own problems she wasn't sure how to let someone else in to help, but for the first time in her life, she was starting to believe that she had found a man worthy of her trust. Alex had done an excellent job of making sure Miss Abigail was protected and cared for. He had done everything that he had promised and hadn't deserted Chelsea, even with a madman trying to kill her. He had even saved her life at the beach this very day. It was time for a leap of faith.

"Okay, Alex. I trust you."

Alex smiled, and his expression showed her that he understood how much those words had cost her. "Thank you." He leaned over and gave her a quick kiss on the cheek. "Okay, look." He pointed down the street to a row of signs that advertised the assorted businesses on the road. "Do you see that hotel up there with the crown on the sign?"

Chelsea followed his motion. "You mean the Royal Palms? Yes, I see it."

"Well that's a five-star hotel. They're bound to have taxis waiting for their guests. All we need to do is get over there without being seen. Think we can do that?"

The gray sedan pulled into a parking lot about two hundred yards ahead and Chelsea squeezed Alex's hand again. The car was right between them and the path to the hotel. "He stopped. He's waiting for us."

Alex shook his head. "He doesn't know where we are, or where we're going. He just knows we're in the vicinity because we left the hotel on foot. Give him a minute. He'll probably start driving again."

As if on cue, the gray car pulled out of the parking lot, turned and came toward them again. Chelsea let out a sigh of relief when it passed them and turned at the corner.

"Okay, let's move." Alex took Chelsea's hand and led her away from the bushes. They crossed the street and sprinted toward the hotel, just as the gray car apparently made a U-turn and appeared back onto the street only a couple of blocks behind them. Two taxis were parked out front. Alex waved a handful of cash as they approached, immediately catching the attention of the drivers that were both leaning against their cars, engrossed in a conversation.

"Someone's chasing us. Here's five hundred bucks for the guy who can lose him and get us to the pier before the next ferry leaves."

The shorter of the two drivers jumped. "I can do that. Hop in."

Alex threw his bag into the backseat, then followed Chelsea in just as the gray car pulled into the valet parking area. With wheels spinning, the cab peeled out of the parking lot, leaving the gray car suddenly stuck behind two hotel vans. It didn't stay stuck long, however, and Alex could see the car pulling out to follow them.

"The guy following us is in that gray car that's just leaving the hotel. See him?"

"Yeah, I see him," the cabbie replied. He caught Alex's eye in the rearview mirror. "You sure you got five hundred bucks?"

"Absolutely," Alex said quickly. He fanned out the bills in his hand so that the amount was visible and showed it to the driver. "But you've got to get us away from that gray car first."

"Not a problem." He turned the wheel and the cab swerved and bolted around the car in front of it, then turned left across the oncoming traffic only narrowly missing a collision with a red pizza delivery truck. Chelsea's eyes grew large and she grabbed Alex's hand as the force of the turn threw her into the seat. The tires squealed against the pavement.

"Maybe seat belts would be a good idea," she said, her voice barely above a whisper.

"I think maybe you're right." He released her hand long enough for both of them to buckle up, then took her hand again as the cab turned right. The cabbie obviously knew the neighborhood, but the gray car still appeared behind them again, causing their driver to spit in disgust.

"This man is like glue. What's he want you for anyway?"

"It's a long story," Alex said. "But I can tell you that if he catches us, it won't be pretty."

"Don't worry," the cabbie said as he jerked the wheel again, forcing the cab to make a hard left just as the gray car was getting closer. "I grew up here. I know every back street and alley in this town."

"That's what we're counting on."

Tires squealed as the chase continued. Alex motioned for Chelsea to sit low on the seat while he kept his eyes on the other car. He still couldn't make out the features of the driver, but he had noticed the man was wearing dark glasses and seemed to have collar-length brown hair. The cab's engine roared as the car bolted and swerved down the busy street. A few moments later the gray car got stuck behind some traffic. Alex's face registered his surprise as their pursuer pulled onto the sidewalk and crashed into a hot dog stand, then continued the chase as bits of metal and food fell away from his car. The driver was obviously determined and wasn't giving up easily.

"The pier is only a few more miles ahead, but I'm going to backtrack to throw him off."

Alex nodded to the cabbie. "Sounds like a plan. Our ferry leaves in ten minutes. Think we can still make it?"

The cabbie shrugged nonchalantly as if he drove in a car chase every afternoon. "For five hundred bucks, I can guarantee it." He slowed and veered to the right, then turned and went down a narrow alley. The cab barely seemed to fit, but there was no one in their path and they suddenly emerged onto another busy street. He punched the gas and the cab shot forward, just as the gray car turned into the alley behind them.

They went less than a block and turned again, this time veering around a mound of construction supplies and other road equipment. They squeaked past a bull-dozer just as it backed into the road, blocking off the gray car that had once again come up behind them.

"There you go," the cabbie said, quite pleased with himself.

Chelsea sat up in the seat and looked behind them. They gray car was indeed blocked and the driver was laying on the horn. A few minutes later they saw the gray car try to back up, but another construction ve-hicle blocked it from behind.

"That should buy us a few minutes," Alex said as he ran his hand through his hair.

The cabbie smiled and turned back into the busy

street that led to the pier. "Never underestimate the local boys."

Within minutes, the cabbie pulled up in front of the ferry station at the pier. Alex and Chelsea got out with their bags and Alex leaned into the driver's window. "Thanks." He handed the man the cash. "You never saw us, right?"

"Right-o," the cabbie said with a smile. He counted the bills, folded them and put them in his pocket. *"Mahalo."* He sped off as Alex took Chelsea's hand and headed for the ferry entrance. The cars were already loaded on the bottom decks and they were now loading the last of the passengers. A conductor motioned for them to hurry and then closed and locked the gate behind them just as they stepped onto the boat.

"Whew, that was close," Chelsea said, her eyes darting back toward the ferry station. Suddenly she tensed involuntarily and ducked behind Alex. "He's here. The man from the hotel."

Alex saw him on the dock as the ferry pushed off and started its voyage toward Maui. He touched Chelsea's waist and moved her farther into the crowd on the boat. The man was looking around and checking his watch, but he didn't seem to have noticed them. He spoke to one of the men at the dock and pointed toward the ferry, but the man was shaking his head.

"I think we're safe," Alex said softly in her ear.

"For now," Chelsea agreed. "Do you think he knows we're on this boat?"

Alex shrugged. "I don't think he knows for sure, but he'll probably figure it out before too long." He motioned with his head. "Let's find a quiet spot, if there is one, and catch our breath."

They made their way through the crowd toward the front of the ferry and passed a man selling snacks and drinks. Chelsea heard her stomach grumble and realized she hadn't had anything to eat since breakfast. "Want anything?" she asked.

"Maybe," Alex said as he followed her over. The vendor didn't have any hot food, but there was a large supply of fresh fruit and deli sandwiches. They made their selections and paid, then headed over to a corner of the ferry that was relatively empty.

Chelsea dug out a small pocketknife from her purse and peeled back a part of the mango she had purchased. "When I was growing up we'd go to the mango groves and pick hundreds of these and carry them around in large wicker baskets. Then we'd suck the juice out of them all summer long while my mom made mango compote and mango ice cream. It's one of my favorite memories."

"Was that in Brazil?" Alex asked as he removed the wrapping from his turkey sandwich.

Chelsea nodded. "A lot of mango trees grow in southern Brazil and we even had one in our backyard. The tree gave us quite a bit of fruit. My mother liked to garden and we always had a lot of different fruits and vegetables growing year 'round."

Alex gave her a smile, realizing that he was truly interested in her family instead of just trying to uncover details for his private investigator to research. He also noticed that it was the first time she had ever volunteered any information about herself. The thought pleased him immensely. He hoped it meant she was starting to believe in their friendship.

She put another piece of fruit in her mouth and

smiled from ear to ear. "I love jaboticaba! I can't believe I found some over here!"

He raised an eyebrow and she rewarded his interest by putting three small round pieces of fruit in his hand. They were about the size and shape of red seedless grapes, but their skin was a dark rich purple that was almost black. "What are these?"

"Another type of fruit from Brazil. They're great." She took another piece of the fruit from the basket and held it up. "You don't eat the skin. You kind of suck out the meat inside, but there is a seed, so be careful." She demonstrated by biting a small hole in the skin, then sucking the white flesh of the fruit into her mouth.

Alex tried to follow her example but he ended up with a piece of skin in his mouth that was very bitter. He grimaced. "Are you sure this is a good idea?"

Chelsea laughed. "Nobody I know has died from it yet. You really don't want to eat the skin, though. Just try the white part of the fruit inside." She demonstrated again, and this time he did it without getting the skin in his mouth.

"What do you think?"

Alex shrugged. "It's okay, I guess. I think I like seedless grapes more and more. They're a lot less trouble."

Chelsea grabbed a few more and ate them, her face radiating happiness. Alex was delighted that she had found something from home that gave her comfort and took her mind away from the danger for even a few minutes. "Well, at least you tried them," Chelsea said. "Now you know what they taste like. I like trying new things. Don't you?"

"It depends," Alex said carefully. "There's a lot to be said for going with the known instead of the unknown."

Chelsea laughed. "That sounds rather boring." She squeezed his arm playfully.

"It also sounds safe."

She ate another piece of fruit. "Do you ever color outside the lines, Alex? Do something on a whim?"

"Spontaneity is not my friend," Alex said quietly. "I'm a planner and I spend so much time working that I rarely have time to try something new."

She seemed to consider this for a moment. "So have you always wanted to be a lawyer?"

Alex took his sandwich apart, squeezed some mustard onto the bread, then put it back together again and took a bite. He was hungrier than he'd thought and his stomach rumbled. "It always seemed interesting to me. My father was a lawyer and he used to take me to the office with him quite a bit. It was exciting to see him helping people with their problems. My love growing up was always baseball, though. I played all through high school and college."

"You must have been a good player," Chelsea mused.

"Good enough to make the minor leagues. I was a pitcher and had a great fastball," Alex agreed as he popped open his soda can.

"Really? So what happened?"

"What happened was I got injured and couldn't play anymore. I was headed for the majors by most peoples' accounts, but I threw out my arm during a game against the Albuquerque Isotopes. That was the end of my baseball career, so I came back to Florida State for my law degree."

"I'm so sorry. You must really miss playing."

Alex considered her words. "I did at first, but I've been able to help a lot of people by being a lawyer, and I get to work with my brother, which I also enjoy."

"I imagine being a lawyer pays a little better, too."

Alex smiled. "Better than the minor leagues, at any rate. But I don't do it for the money. I mean, of course I want to get paid for the work I do, but I get a real sense of satisfaction when a case ends well. That's more important than the paycheck to me. I'm probably one of the few people that can honestly say I love my work." For the first time in quite a while he felt truly content.

He leaned forward and tucked her hair behind her ear. She was so beautiful, even with the lines of stress around her eyes and the roughness in her voice from her close call at the beach. He quickly collected their trash from the meal, then returned and sat beside her on the bench, gently pulling her back to lean against him. He felt her relax and noticed how well she fit in his arms. The more he knew about this lady, the more he liked. He couldn't accept that she would disappear from his life forever after Miss Abigail's surgery. Somehow he had to convince her to stay. No matter if she called herself Chelsea or Cecilia, this woman in front of him was slowly weaving herself into his heart.

Chelsea chewed on her bottom lip, finally feeling calm enough to sort through her problem with Justin Carver with careful thought instead of just reacting in a panic. She sighed, buoyed by the comfort of Alex's arms. He believed in her, and helped her to feel a confidence that had completely disappeared from her life over the past month of running. Could he truly help her, as he promised? Could the computer expert he mentioned really gain access to Carver's files? Could he help her find the forensic accountant that she needed? Surely if they worked together...

Her brain seemed fuzzy with exhaustion, but the thought of fighting back against Carver helped her to feel a new wave of optimism. She closed her eyes, ready to talk through the possibilities with Alex once they had a chance to rest and regroup. Her heart warmed at the thought. Her feelings for him were growing exponentially, and for the first time in her life, she felt the buds of tenderness and trust growing in her heart. She clung to the sliver of hope as she drifted off to sleep.

FIFTEEN

The ferry trip to Maui took about two hours, and both Alex and Chelsea dozed on and off during the voyage. A fog horn blasted as the ferry approached the dock and the sound startled them both awake. Passengers all around them readied themselves to disembark and gathered their belongings.

Alex pulled out his cell phone and checked to see if he had any messages. He didn't, but he noticed that the power light indicated that he had dropped a bar. He turned off his phone, knowing that he wouldn't have a way to charge it anytime in the near future but would still need it to keep in touch with Abigail's doctor and to call his brother Dominic again once they got settled into a hotel. He pocketed the phone, then smiled at Chelsea who was wiping the sleep out of her eyes.

"Ready to go?"

"As ready as I'll ever be. Do you think more men will be waiting for us at the dock?"

"Hard to say," Alex answered. "Let's try to stay in the middle of the group of passengers and keep our heads down. There must be five hundred people on this ferry. It shouldn't be that hard to blend in and keep hidden."

Chelsea followed Alex's lead as they hid themselves among the passengers, keeping a vigilant watch for anyone suspicious. They didn't see anyone who looked familiar, but Carver had a huge amount of resources, so she doubted that the two burly men they'd faced before were their only threat.

They saw two men at the edge of the crowd standing close together and surveying the disembarking passengers. Chelsea didn't recognize either of them, but their stance and demeanor was similar to the men that had been chasing them in Oahu. Chelsea grabbed Alex's hand and squeezed it, then nodded toward the men to show him her concern. He nodded back and they slowly made their way away from the men, trying to be as inconspicuous as possible. Fear made Chelsea's stomach clench, but having Alex by her side helped to strengthen her resolve and feel a new sense of confidence. She kept her head down and eyes lowered so she wouldn't call attention to herself. Once a good distance away she dared a look back, but the two men were looking in a different direction and she breathed out a sigh of relief.

A few minutes later they quickly made their way to a taxi and asked to be taken to a mid-priced hotel near the hospital in Kahului. Alex rented two adjoining rooms again and soon they were safely ensconced inside. He tossed his duffel bag onto the bed and turned to Chelsea.

"Are you going to be able to sleep?"

"I'm going to give it my best shot. I'm exhausted even with that nap on the ferry."

"Well, you've probably had better days." He cupped her face with his hands and looked deeply into her eyes. When he spoke, his voice was soft yet insistent. "No running without me, right?"

She gave him a tired smile. "Right, counselor. I'm not going anywhere tonight."

He smiled in response and just stared into her eyes for a moment. Then, without thinking, he bent to give her a kiss on the lips that felt like the most natural thing in the world. Her response was tentative at first, but grew stronger as tingles shot down his spine. Her lips were soft and reminded him of rose petals. This woman was special. How was he going to let her go tomorrow?

She broke the kiss and took a step back. He noticed a slight blush to her cheeks. It made her even more beautiful.

"Good night, Chelsea."

"Good night, Alex." She walked to the door that separated the two rooms, then turned to face him. "Thank you for today. Thank you for saving my life and sticking by me."

"You're welcome." Her words were sincere, but seemed tinged by a hint of sadness. Was she already planning her escape?

The alarm jolted Alex awake the next morning and he grabbed the clock, trying to hit the snooze button. It was just past seven in the morning. He hadn't meant to sleep that long, but had set the alarm as a backup just in case he didn't wake up at his normal six o'clock. He reached for his cell phone and turned it on, then checked his messages. He'd had a call from his brother Dominic and he quickly hit the button to dial his brother's number.

"Sullivan," Dominic answered.

"How's life in the big city?" Alex asked, repeating an inside joke they'd had between them for years.

"Hey, big brother," Dominic said, his voice anxious. "My boss says you have a serious problem and need some help. What can I do for you?"

Alex could hear that his brother was tired, but he also knew that Dominic would help him with whatever he asked, no matter what he had on his own plate. All three of the Sullivan brothers had a very tight relationship. If the chips were down, they always knew they could count on one another for help. "Do you have a few minutes? It's kind of a long story."

"I have as long as you need, Alex. Start at the beginning, and don't leave out a thing."

Alex smiled. "All right. You asked for it." He started pacing as he talked, beginning with Miss Abigail's first convincing him to jump on the plane to Maui. He didn't stop for more than an hour as they discussed the situation. Dominic asked questions here and there, but for the most part, he let Alex tell the story without interruption.

When Alex was finished bringing his brother up to speed, he sat down on the bed, drained. It felt good to share the burden with Dominic, even though he was miles away. "So what should we do now?" he asked.

Dominic was silent for a moment, then answered. "Give me an hour or so to make some calls. I have a buddy that works up at the Chicago Police Department. He helped us with an interstate case a while back. I'll give him a shout, and a few others. Can you stay put where you are?"

"Yes, I think we're safe here. We've been here all night, and if Carver knew where we were, I doubt he would have waited to come after us."

"All right. Stay put and stay safe. I'll call you back as soon as I can."

Alex hung up and rubbed the sleep out of his eyes, then headed for the shower. A few minutes later, somewhat refreshed, he started riffling through their purchases from the day before, looking for something to eat. This hotel certainly didn't have room service, but it did offer a continental breakfast. For a moment Alex considered going downstairs to pick up some food. He ultimately decided against it for safety reasons and opted for a bag of powdered sugar doughnuts they had bought the day before. The room also had a coffeemaker, so he started brewing a pot as he munched on a few of the sugary confections.

He finished with the coffee and glanced at the clock. It was almost nine. Miss Abigail had gone into surgery at seven-thirty, so he figured he could call in another half hour or so for a preliminary report from the doctor. So far there were no messages from the doctor on his phone, so he assumed no news was good news. He was considering his next move when his cell phone buzzed. The caller ID said it was Dominic, and he answered quickly, eager to find out what his brother had discovered.

The two men talked for a while before Alex heard a knock at the adjoining door and Chelsea poked her head inside. Alex motioned her in, then finished his call and flipped the phone closed. Her hair was mussed and her face was still puffy with sleep, but Alex thought she had never looked lovelier.

"Did you sleep well?" he asked softly.

"Not really. I kept thinking about that madman at the beach and it was pretty scary. I must have slept a little, though, because all of a sudden I woke up and it was morning."

Alex touched her face and drew his hand down her cheek. "I'm sorry. I wish I could have done something to help you sleep better."

"I appreciate that." She gave him a smile. "Do we know anything new?"

Alex took her hand and led her over to a chair. "I just got off the phone with my brother Dominic back in Tallahassee. He's got law enforcement in Chicago trying to locate Carver. As a side note, you should know that they are very interested in what you have to say. Carver's office reports that he's out of town. Based on everything that's happened, I'm thinking the odds are he's here in Maui."

Chelsea gasped and covered her face with her hands. "I was afraid of that," she whispered. "Somehow I knew, even though I didn't want to believe it."

Alex sat down on the bed. "Well, Dominic's advice is to lay low for a few hours while he gets some men over here that he can trust to take care of you. Maui is so small that they don't have any U.S. Marshals here, so they're flying over a couple of guys from Honolulu. Hopefully, in a few hours we'll have some help. They'll take you into protective custody and get you back over to the mainland. He told me they'd call my cell phone once they arrive."

Chelsea's face was troubled. "Do you trust him?"

With Chelsea's history, Alex wasn't surprised or offended by the question. "I do, Chelsea. My brother is an honorable man. He's also careful, and he does his job well. Since Carver's actions have been interstate, he had no problem getting the marshals to take jurisdiction and open an investigation. He's on your side."

Chelsea closed her eyes and rubbed her temples. "Unbelievable."

"What do you mean?"

Chelsea didn't answer for a moment and just sat there with her eyes closed. Finally she opened them and the look she gave him was pure frustration and weariness. "Don't get me wrong, I'm thankful for the help. It's just never going to end, you know? Just when I thought I was finally getting my life back together, it all shattered into little pieces all over again. I'm never going to be able to live a normal life without looking over my shoulder."

"Yes, you will," Alex said forcefully. "It may take a while, but you're strong. You're going to make it through this."

She gave him a weary smile. "Well, I'm not going to make it anywhere without a shower to help get me going this morning." She sniffed. "Is that coffee I smell?"

"Absolutely." Alex grinned. "I'm not much of a cook, but I can make a pot of coffee." He grabbed the bag of doughnuts and held it out to her. "I also spent all morning making these wonderful doughnuts for you. I hope you like powdered sugar. It's my specialty—an old family recipe."

She laughed and held up her hands. "Oh, no. I'm not ready for that yet. First things first. I have got to take a shower to get my engine running." She paused a moment, then sheepishly grabbed a doughnut with an impish grin and headed back to her room.

About half an hour later the two sat at the small table sharing a simple breakfast of doughnuts and coffee. Alex's cell phone rang yet again and he answered it quickly, had a short conversation and closed his phone with a snap.

"That was Miss Abigail's doctor," he said with a smile on his face. "Miss Abigail's surgery went extremely well and there were no complications. She's resting comfortably."

"What wonderful news!" Chelsea said happily. She jumped up and hugged Alex, her relief clearly evident on her face.

Alex pulled back a moment so he could see Chelsea's eyes, then cupped her face and gently touched her lips with his thumbs. Her skin was incredibly soft. He leaned forward and kissed her. It was a tentative kiss at first, just like the first one, but grew stronger as she responded. Fire shot from his fingertips all the way down to his toes.

The knock on the door startled them both. They quickly stepped apart and Chelsea touched her lips with her fingers, a look of fear replacing the happiness that had been there only seconds before.

Alex went over to the door and cautiously looked out the peephole. A man in a dark suit was standing there. As Alex watched, he looked at his watch and tapped his foot impatiently. Alex motioned Chelsea over to the door and had her look at the man, as well.

"Do you recognize him?" Alex whispered.

Chelsea shook her head, her eyes round with fear.

"He looks vaguely familiar, but after the past few days I've had and everything that's happened, I can't place him."

"Hide, then!" Alex ordered softly. "Go back into your room until I know who this guy is and why he's here. If you hear anything suspicious at all, get as far away from here as you can. Then call me on my cell and we'll rendezvous later." The man knocked again and the noise seemed to startle Chelsea out of her trance. With a quick motion she ran through the door that separated the two rooms. Alex heard the lock click behind her.

"Mr. Sullivan?"

Alex could hear the man's muffled voice and was surprised that the stranger knew his name. He looked through the peephole again and this time the man was holding up a badge to the small window. "Police, Mr. Sullivan. I need you to open the door."

Alex opened the door a few inches and studied the man's badge. It seemed real enough.

"I'm John Shepard, Maui police. I was told you had a witness with you—a Ms. Chelsea Rogers. I'm here to take her into protective custody."

Alex opened the door a little wider and motioned for the man to enter, then closed the door soundly behind him. He turned and eyed the man carefully. The newcomer was slightly shorter than Alex, but was heavily muscled and probably lived at the gym. He was clean-shaved and his hair was neatly trimmed, but he had two dark bruises on his face. His eyes were dark and calculating, and he dressed quite a bit better than any of the law-enforcement officers Alex had ever met. Of course, the dress code was flexible in different situations, and the clothes alone didn't signal any dishonesty on the man's part. The problem was the timing. He wasn't expecting anyone from the U.S. Marshals for a couple of hours, and they were also supposed to call his cell phone before arriving. How had the local police even gotten pulled into the mix? Had Dominic called them but forgotten to mention it? Alex considered his options; not missing the bulge on the man's left side where the shoulder holster held his gun.

"How did you find us?" Alex asked cautiously.

"We got a call from the federal marshals and told them we'd be happy to help them out and keep an eye on Ms. Rogers until they got here. We're expecting backup in a couple of hours, but my assignment is to keep Ms. Rogers safe until we can get her back to the office, and ultimately, over to the mainland." He shifted and his eyes surveyed the room. "Did she go next door?"

Alex felt a mixture of emotions swimming inside him. Was this man for real? He didn't want to stand in the way of Chelsea's safety, but he also didn't want to turn her over to someone else, especially someone he didn't know. Her problems had become his, and he felt a strong urge to protect her.

"Can I stay with her?"

Shepard shook his head. "That's not possible. You'd put her in danger. I need to get her to a safe house as quickly as I can. Another person would slow us down and make us more vulnerable if a dangerous situation arose."

Although the words made sense, a warning bell seemed to go off in the back of Alex's mind. The officer's eyes were narrowed and he seemed to be ill at ease and ready to pounce. Alex studied him a little closer and a feeling of wrongness suddenly overwhelmed him. His cell phone still hadn't rung, and Dominic had promised him a call. His brother was a careful, detail-oriented marshal. Alex doubted he would have forgotten to mention that he had brought in the local police if including them had really been the plan.

Shepard seemed to realize that his cover was blown. Before Alex could even react, the imposter pulled out a 9 mm pistol and hit Alex on the temple with the butt of the gun.

A flash of pain shot through Alex's head and dizziness swamped him, but he reached out and tried to grab for the gun, sending both men into a table with a large crash. From there, they wrestled each other into the wall, smashing a floor lamp and a framed wall print to the floor. The imposter moved incredibly fast and seemed to anticipate both Alex's defense and offense. An uppercut caught Alex's jaw, and another strike caught his nose. Alex landed a blow on the man's abdomen, but got two in return in rapid succession. His opponent's combat skills were impressive, and Alex knew he was outmatched, yet he couldn't give up. Chelsea was counting on him.

He swung at the man's head and his fist was deflected, but his second punch caught the stranger hard in the gut. The man grunted and took a step backward, but he recovered quickly and landed another punch on Alex's nose. Alex felt the blood drip down his face, but connected again with a strike to the man's chin. He followed with another punch to the imposter's left eye.

Unfortunately that was the last punch Alex was able

to land. The imposter caught Alex hard in the nose a second time, and before Alex could regroup, another blow caught him in the stomach and forced him back against the dresser. He bumped his head on the edge of the furniture and the room started spinning as he hit the floor.

Shepard quickly stepped around Alex's body and headed to the door that led to the adjoining room. It was locked, but he rammed it with his shoulder and the lock broke free.

Alex tried to stand and follow him so he could keep Chelsea safe, but a wave of vertigo swept over him and he hit the floor again, barely able to see the man as he slowly opened the door and scanned the room for the woman.

"Ms. Rogers? Police. My orders are to take you into protective custody." As he spoke Shepard searched the room, his gun still drawn.

Alex finally made it to his knees and was able to make it to the door frame just in time to see the aggressor open the closet door quickly, pointing his weapon inside.

It must have been empty because he quickly moved into the bathroom; Alex could hear him pulling back the shower curtain. "Ms. Rogers? I'm here to help you." Finding nothing, he returned and checked under the beds, then grunted before leaving, slamming the door behind him and leaving Alex struggling for consciousness on the floor.

One thought hit Alex as the room swirled around him.

Chelsea Rogers was gone.

SIXTEEN

A few minutes later Alex slowly pulled himself back into his room, his head pounding so badly he could barely think. He pinched his nose, trying to stop the bleeding. His nose was definitely broken. He took a few deep breaths, his thoughts slowly coming into focus and a sense of emptiness enveloping him. Chelsea was gone. Had the fake policeman caught up to her away from the hotel, or had she successfully escaped? When his cell phone rang, it took him a couple of seconds to even react. Finally, on the fifth ring, he flipped it open and answered.

"Sullivan."

"Alex. Are you okay?"

Alex instantly reacted to Chelsea's voice and sat up quickly. His head pounded from the quick movement and he groaned. "Where are you?" he asked tightly.

"I'm safe. Should I call an ambulance? I heard the fight through the hotel wall."

"No!" Alex answered in a frustrated tone, his pride getting the better of him. "Tell me where you are and I'll come get you."

Chelsea paused. "No, Alex, I don't think that's a

good idea. I'm so sorry that man hurt you. Are you sure you're going to be okay?"

Alex dragged a hand slowly over his face, the mixed emotions weighing heavily on him. He could understand her hesitance. He had failed her and hadn't kept her safe. Now he could lose her forever. "Chelsea, please. I know I let you down. Please give me another chance. We can fight Carver and his cohorts together through legal channels. Those men from the marshal's office will be here any minute. They can keep you safe. Don't go it alone."

"I have to, Alex." She took a deep breath and her voice wavered as she spoke the next words. "You didn't let me down, but this has to be goodbye. Thank you for everything. You've been wonderful. I really mean it. I enjoyed my time with you. Please take care of Miss Abigail, okay?"

Alex hit the floor with his fist, his own voice filled with frustration. "No, it's not okay, and this is not the end. I'm worried about you. Don't shut me out."

Alex could tell she was crying but trying to control it. When she spoke, her voice was raspy. "Listen, Alex. You really helped me out. Now I have a plan, a real plan, for proving Carver is guilty of the embezzlement. I have that program we downloaded, and I'll find a computer expert to help me out once I get back to the mainland. When I get the files I need, I'll save my money until I can hire a forensic accountant to sort everything out. I really think it will work, and I never could have gotten this far without you. Thank you so much for all of your help."

Alex was glad that she had a plan and that he'd played at least a small part in helping her fight back, yet he was taken aback by the fact that she was still try-ing to end their relationship. "What if I don't want to forget about you? What if I want you in my life? Chel-sea, we can work this out. Dominic and the marshal's office are going to help us. We'll get this Carver situa-tion figured out together. Please don't end it like this." He swallowed hard. "Let me help you."

There was silence at the end of the phone for a moment—then finally she spoke. "Please, go back to Tallahassee, Alex. Forget you even met me. I'll be all right. I can make it on my own and start over some-where new. And I'll pay you back for the money you gave me from the bank yesterday. It may take me a while, but I promise I'll send it to you as soon as I can."

"I'm not worried about the money, Chelsea. Don't do this. You said yourself, Carver is ruthless. Let me help you. Please."

"I can't. Go back to Tallahassee." Her voice was a mere whisper.

"Chelsea, please! Tell me where you are!" Alex's tone was desperate now, but he heard the click and knew she was no longer on the line. Before he could even put the phone away, it was ringing again.

The voice on the other end was no-nonsense and deep. "This is Delaney from the U.S. Marshal's office. We're en route to Maui and will be arriving at approxi-mately 12:35 p.m. We want you to stay at your current location until we get there."

A cold fear settled in Alex's heart. "She's gone."

"What do you mean 'she's gone'? Tell me what hap-pened."

"A man named Shepard claiming to be from the

local police department tried to pick her up just a little while ago."

"Hold a minute."

Alex waited for what seemed like an eternity for Delaney to come back on the line. When he did, the marshal's voice was heavy. "There is no law enforcement officer named Shepard anywhere in or near the Hawaiian Islands. Tell me what he looked like and exactly what happened."

With mounting exasperation, Alex went through the details of the past half hour, all the while a cold fear ran up his spine. A ruthless killer could be stalking Chelsea at this very moment, and Alex hadn't been able to stop him. Guilt assailed him again and he slowly pulled himself to his feet and sank heavily into a chair. He'd gotten his nose to stop bleeding, but blood still dripped from the wound on his temple. He swiped it out of his eyes.

When he finally hung up with the agent, he was completely drained. He clipped his cell phone on his hip and grabbed what few belongings he had with him, stuffing them into his duffel bag. She could be anywhere on the island by now, but Alex was going to do his best to find her before it was too late. If anything happened to her... He couldn't bear the thought. He paused for a moment, knowing what he needed to do. This problem was too big for him to handle alone. Only God could help protect Chelsea. What was that Bible verse? What man means for evil, God can use for good? He knelt by the bed, his heart wide-open, and prayed fervently for Chelsea's safety.

Chelsea looked over the top of the book she was pretending to read. Her position, seated at the end of the health and fitness aisle of the bookstore, was perfect for watching the front door for anyone suspicious. The more she thought about it, the more she realized that the assailant at the hotel had been the same man in the gray car that had been chasing them yesterday in Oahu. He had cut his hair, shaved and put on a suit, but it had to have been him. She wished she had recognized him sooner so she could have warned Alex, but there had just been too much happening in the past few days to keep it all straight.

She leaned against a cushion as her thoughts raced, even as her body was nearing exhaustion. Was it only yesterday the man had tried to drown her? She closed her eyes and said a small prayer for strength. The pain in her heart from leaving Alex behind was worse than she'd anticipated, yet she knew without a doubt that she had done the right thing. He'd been hurt enough on her account.

She turned her thoughts to planning her escape from Maui. Alex had given her enough money to leave the island by plane, but could she even make it to the jetway undetected? For all she knew, Carver's men were combing the entire airport every hour on the hour, and even her new appearance wouldn't keep them from recognizing her. They would expect her to fly, and the airport would be the first place they'd look. No, she needed a different plan. Maybe she could take one of the ferries or charter boats to one of the other islands and fly to the mainland from one of those airports. Or maybe it was better to just hole up somewhere on Maui for a few weeks and let Carver's men think she had left.

A wave of nervousness ran through her and she shivered involuntarily. Everything was happening too fast.

What she needed was time to rest and to think, time to weigh out the various options, and time to plan her next move. Unfortunately time was a luxury she didn't have.

She bit her bottom lip as her mind spun through the various possibilities. So far the boat idea seemed the best, but was taking a ferry even practical? She knew there were two other islands fairly close by, and Oahu had a decent-size airport. Did it make sense to hop over Oahu or should she try a different island? She considered her options, but the only other way off Maui that came to mind was by helicopter, and there was no way she was flying in one of those death traps. She moaned inwardly. There simply weren't a lot of different options when it came to leaving the island. This was a fact she was sure hadn't escaped Carver's men, either.

A wave of hopelessness swept over her. Was escape even possible? She felt like a trapped animal, with hunters just waiting to move in for the kill. Despite everything, a small part of her wanted to call Alex and have him with her so they could face these problems together. It had been so nice to share her burden with him, even if it had been for such a short time. He had truly been the first man in her life who hadn't let her down. The fact that she was starting to have feelings for him scared her right down to her toes. How could she ever have a relationship with anyone until Carver was behind bars, though? The answer was simple. She couldn't.

The practical aspects hit her hard, as well. She had no idea how long it would take her to prove Carver's guilt. Alex had a successful legal firm and a life in Tallahassee, neither of which he would want to put on indefinite hold while she pursued the case against Carver.

Even if Alex cared about her now, if she dragged him away from his life then he would probably soon grow to resent her for everything he had given up to be with her. She hated to lose him and the possibility of getting to know him better, but she didn't see any way that she could have a relationship with him without putting his life and happiness in jeopardy.

She wondered briefly if Alex had met up with the U.S. Marshals that had come over to help protect her. Could she try to reach out to them directly? The arguments warred within her. A small part of her wanted to trust law enforcement to help, but after everything that had happened with her father and even the police in Oahu, she just couldn't take that leap. She just couldn't trust law enforcement, even if Alex's brother was as dependable as he claimed.

But could she keep herself safe alone? Should she? She had been an accountant before Carver entered her life, not a policewoman or some other job that would have given her the proper training to escape a threat like Carver. Was she fooling herself into believing she could actually win against Carver?

She stood, walked over to the local tourist section of the bookstore and started thumbing through one of the guidebooks, hoping to find the ferry schedule.

"May I help you find something?" the young attendant was friendly looking and gave her a helpful smile.

"Yes, I'm hoping to find out about the ferries that go between the islands."

The woman thought for a moment, then pulled out a guidebook. "This is probably the best one. There are two major docks on Maui, one at Kahului and one at Lahaina. The one at Kahului doesn't have much to offer tourists and is used more for shipping, but you'll probably find what you're looking for at Lahaina."

Chelsea flipped through the pages. They'd come in on the ferry at Lahaina last night, but it was a good distance away from where she was now. "It looks like most of the boats leaving the docks are tourist trips taking day excursions for fishing or snorkeling. Is that the case?"

The attendant frowned, picked up another copy of the same book and glanced at the index, then turned to a section in the back. "Ah, here you go. There are a lot of those tourist trips, but you can also get to the island of Lanai by ferry. That island lies to the southwest of Maui." She showed Chelsea where to find the information and smiled. "Is there anything else I can help you with?"

"No, thanks. I appreciate your time." Chelsea watched her leave and then turned back to the book. If she could just get to Lanai City in the middle of the island, she could catch a flight to Honolulu. There were two large hotels there if she got caught waiting for a flight and, according to the guidebook, several bed-and-breakfast establishments. Any of those would serve her purposes if she ended up having to wait before she could catch a flight to the mainland. She flipped through a few more pages and found the ferry schedule.

She kept turning pages to see if she had any other options. Another ferry traveled from Lahaina to Molokai, an island to the northwest of Maui. If she could get to Hoolehua, the major city on Molokai, she could catch a plane from there to Honolulu, as well. She breathed a sigh of relief as her plan took shape. All she needed to do was to get to the Lahaina harbor and find the ferry with the largest crowd going to either location so she could blend in among the tourists.

Chelsea pulled open a map of Maui. Lahaina was several miles away from Kahului, so taking a taxi would probably cost a small fortune. She didn't think any local buses were an option, and hitching a ride sounded absolutely insane. Somehow, she needed to get a car and make it to the Lahaina harbor. Once there, she could disappear into the crowds once and for all.

She concentrated on what she'd do then, all the steps she'd take moving forward. The planning kept her feeling calm and centered—and it distracted her from thoughts of the man she was leaving behind.

SEVENTEEN

Alex threw his duffel on the bed and turned to watch the marshals set up their communications equipment. Once the deputies had arrived a little after lunch, they had met up with Alex and moved to a different hotel to set up a command post.

Normally they would have sent Alex on his way once they had debriefed him, but apparently Deputy Delaney had liked Alex's no-nonsense attitude and decided to let him stay, hoping that Chelsea might try to contact him by cell phone. They had found a charger for him and asked for him to keep the phone on just in case.

The local police force was finally playing ball now that the feds had arrived, and Deputy Delaney had managed to have the local airport and docks covered with surveillance. He had also rigged up a system to track Chelsea by her cell phone if she ever decided to turn it on, and had started running checks with the local hotels and tourist companies in case she tried to leave Maui. The only problem was that Carver's men were probably doing the exact same thing, so Alex knew the big question was who would get to Chelsea first.

He was also feeling guilty—because now he knew that Carver had probably been tracking his cell phone all along, which was how his men had been able to trace them to the hotels. He'd kept it on all morning to make sure Miss Abigail's doctor could reach him, but he should have come up with a different way to communicate that hadn't put Chelsea in danger. Thankfully, he had given Chelsea a brand-new throwaway cell, so they wouldn't have her number or a way to track her. Unfortunately the good guys couldn't track her, either, even though they had her number, since she'd apparently turned it off after she had called him to say goodbye.

Alex stood and stretched, then joined Delaney by the coffeepot and poured himself a cup. "Any news?" he asked hopefully.

Delaney shook his head. "So far we can't find her at any of the local hotels, and no one seems to recognize her from the circular we've been distributing. Either Carver already has her, or she's better at hiding than I gave her credit for."

Alex's gut clenched at Delaney's words. The marshal had given him more background on Carver, and all of it twisted his stomach. Carver was ruthless. He was also heavily into retribution and revenge toward anyone who interfered with his plans. After all that he had learned, Alex knew without a doubt that Carver wouldn't stop hunting Chelsea until she was dead. He said another silent prayer for her safety, then sat wearily on the edge of the bed. Her smile and her inner beauty had touched him as no one had before. He couldn't imagine life without her.

Dear Lord, please keep her safe. Please bring her back to me.

Chelsea adjusted her duffel bag and took a deep breath as she surveyed the dock. There were about a hundred people milling about, and she was suddenly filled with second thoughts. Maybe this boat idea hadn't been so great, after all. She had hoped for bigger crowds, but with this small number of tourists, she felt entirely too conspicuous. One of the more popular tour companies had a large open air area set up with picnic tables and check-in desks and she migrated toward the larger groups, hoping to blend in with the sightseers.

She had been pleased with her success so far at keeping undetected. On her walk to the closest car rental lots, she had come across a young mother pushing her baby in a stroller. Fifty bucks and a smile later and the woman had agreed to drive her to Lahaina with no questions asked.

Now, however, all of her clever maneuvering seemed for naught. Carver had to have someone keeping an eye on this place. Her stomach was cramping with knots of nervousness. She hoped her new haircut and clothing would give her at least a small chance of boarding one of the ferries undetected.

She waited in the ticket line for the ferry to Lanai that would be leaving in thirty minutes. Hiding behind one of the brochures, she pretended to be interested in the various snorkel trips that were available.

"After you, Ms. Rogers."

She looked up into brown eyes and short-cropped

jet-black hair. The man was wearing khakis and a polo shirt, like a typical tourist, but she saw the holster strap under the flap of his lightweight linen jacket and her muscles tightened involuntarily. He had been so silent in his approach that she hadn't even noticed him come up. Her eyes widened in alarm, but for some reason she didn't think this man was part of Carver's brigade. He was just too neat in appearance, too government-issue. She took a step backward, then another, but he reached out and grabbed her arm before she could run. She pulled against him as fear coursed through her veins.

"Don't make a scene," he warned as his fingers clamped around her arm. "I'm a federal marshal, and I'm here to take you in."

For some reason that news didn't make her feel safe at all. In fact, she'd convinced herself that going it alone was the only hope she had. She still didn't trust law enforcement one iota. "What if I don't want to go in?" she snapped, her eyes darting around her desperately. "What if I don't trust you to keep me safe?"

The marshal pulled her close to stop her struggling. He was holding her so tightly she was sure she'd have bruises from his grip. "You don't have a lot of choice in the matter, Ms. Rogers. Now come with me to the parking lot. We think Carver is on the island, and he's not here as a tourist. You're in grave danger."

Her feet felt like lead and she pulled against him with all of her might. What if he wasn't telling her the truth? A few passersby had noticed their altercation and whispered, seeming to wonder whether or not to interfere. The marshal grimaced and leaned so close that she could smell the mint on his breath. The man locked eyes with her and his glare was so intense that it made her stop struggling.

"Look, lady. I'll cuff you, throw you over my shoulder and carry you out of here if I have to, but that's really not the way I want for this to go down. The bottom line is that Carver probably has a guy staking out this place, too, and if you keep struggling, he's going to be on us like glue. Now get with the program and settle yourself down. Got it? I'm here to help you."

"How do I know you're not with Carver?"

"Because if I were, I'd already have a gun on you."

A cold chill swept through her and she glanced around, noticing the worried expressions of the bystanders. The marshal was right about one thing. She was definitely making a spectacle of herself and drawing more attention than she needed or wanted.

She tried to see the positive side of the situation. Although she hadn't wanted to be found at all, at least being found by the marshals was better than being found by Carver's men. Maybe everything would work out for the best if she gave law enforcement one last chance to help her. The question was, would they believe her story, or would she end up in prison herself due to Carver's lies? She stopped struggling and stood there, limp. Her entire life was spinning out of her control and her options were few.

"Okay," she finally said. She pulled her arm one final time in a motion of defiance, but this time the marshal released her for the sake of the onlookers. He glared at a few of them and they eventually went back to minding their own business.

"I've got a car out in the parking lot. Let's go."

"I want to see your badge first—and your ID."

The man nodded and pulled out his ID case. She looked at it closely, then nodded.

"Okay. Where are we headed?"

"We have a safe house in Kahului that will do just fine until we can get you back to the mainland. We'll take your statement there and begin our investigation."

They left the ticketing area and headed around the shops toward the rows of cars. A few people were milling around, but nobody seemed to pay them any more attention. They turned a corner and Chelsea heard a hard *thunk* and a moan behind her. She turned to see another burly man in jeans and a T-shirt standing over the marshal. He had a gun in his hand and had just hit the marshal from behind. He was reaching to hit him again to make sure he stayed down.

Chelsea didn't have time to think, she just started running. She heard noises behind her, then the sound of footsteps following her, but she didn't have the nerve to look back to see how close her pursuer was to actually catching her. She darted around cars and ran back across the street, barely avoiding being hit by a dark green pickup. Tires screeched and the driver leaned on the horn. She swerved and ran toward a small strip mall. Limbs shaking, she darted behind a wall and paused to catch her breath, her chest heaving with effort. Her heart was pounding so loudly it sounded like a bass drum in a parade and the muscles in her legs burned. Fear coursed through her and she trembled uncontrollably.

Suddenly she felt something small and hard forced into her back and she tensed, wanting to flee again but afraid to even move.

"In case you're wondering, Ms. Rogers, this is a

9 mm automatic that I have pressed against your spine. It's loaded with hollow-tipped bullets. If you don't do exactly as I say, it will blow a hole in you about the size of my fist. Got it?"

Chelsea nodded, pure terror pounding her heartbeat in her ears so loudly she could barely hear his words. The man was so close his breath felt hot upon her neck. Her own breath caught in her throat and she felt light-headed as if she would faint at any moment.

"Okay, lady. Now listen closely. Your friend is out of commission, got it? It's just you and me now. And we're going to walk back over to the parking lot and get into my car. Then we're going for a little ride. Understand? No sudden moves, or I'll take care of you the same way I took care of your friend."

Chelsea nodded, gripping her duffel so hard her knuckles were turning white. The fear she had felt with the marshal had now doubled, making her so shaky she could barely walk.

"Are you with Carver?"

The man's smile was his only response, but it was enough to answer her question. He grabbed her arm and led her to a nearby parking lot, then forced her to get into a gold-colored SUV.

She fought off the panic, trying to take deep breaths. She had to pull herself together and think. There had to be a way out of this mess. If not, she was as good as dead.

Alex sank down into a chair and closed his eyes, the news of Chelsea's abduction hitting him hard. Delaney's man had just called in and filled them in on what had happened at the Lahaina harbor, including the fact that he hadn't seen who had hit him and didn't have a clue as to Chelsea's current whereabouts. The bottom line was that Carver's men had captured her, and Alex didn't know how much time that gave them to find her. He gritted his teeth in frustration. Chelsea was in mortal danger, and he felt totally helpless. How could he lose her now? More importantly, how could he go on without her? He was falling in love with her. It was that simple. And he had wasted all of his time with her with suspicions and doubts instead of seeing her true beauty.

Suddenly his cell phone rang and jerked him out of his thoughts.

"Hello?"

Empty silence met him and he almost hung up before he heard a very faint voice. It sounded distant and he could hear other background noises, but the more he strained, the more he could hear Chelsea's voice and things being moved around, as if she was searching in her duffle for something.

"Why are you taking me to Hana?" Chelsea asked, her voice obviously filled with fear but with an inner strength that he now recognized and admired.

"I'm not taking you to Hana. I'm taking you to Carver. Carver wants the honor of escorting you to Hana himself. He has a little surprise for you. Now just give me that candy bar you promised me and then sit back and be quiet until we get there."

Alex didn't recognize the man's voice, but it obviously wasn't friendly. He heard rustling noises and finally understood what was happening. Somehow Chelsea had managed to rummage around in her bag and turn on her cell phone. She obviously couldn't pick it up and have a normal conversation, but somehow she had been able to speed dial his number without the kidnapper's knowledge. Now she was trying to give him hints about her location inconspicuously. Alex quickly called Delaney on the hotel phone to let him know what was going on, then tried again to focus on Chelsea's conversation with the kidnapper, desperate to pick up as much information as he could.

"What's in Hana?" Chelsea asked, ignoring the man's order for quiet. "The airport is here in Kahului."

The man laughed. "Honey, you don't need to worry about that. What makes you think you're ever leaving this island?"

When Chelsea spoke again, her voice was quavering. "Since when does Carver own a house in Hana?"

"It's not his, it's his uncle's. The Carver family has enough money to have a mansion on every island over here if they want to. And just think. In an hour or so, you'll get a chance to experience the Carver hospitality firsthand. Now, no more questions or I'll have to gag that pretty mouth of yours, understand? Just forget the candy bar and put that bag away." The kidnapper's voice was sinister and Alex silently hoped that Chelsea backed off for a little while so the man wouldn't follow through on his threat. At the same time, he ran through what he knew about Hana in his mind.

The town was fairly small and situated on the far eastern side of the island. He didn't think they had a major airport, but he did know that people rented helicopters to fly to Hana for the bird's eye view of the beautiful waterfalls and rugged coastline. There must be a helicopter pad somewhere and, he thought, they might have a small runway for general aviation.

Although it wasn't on every visitor's list of things to do, the traffic heading to the small town was often congested because the road to Hana was a tourist attraction in itself. Alex didn't know if the traffic on the road would be a hindrance or a help to getting Chelsea back.

The Hana Highway was a narrow strip of pavement that wound along the side of the mountain with barely enough room for a car to pass on several locations. It was fifty-two miles long but took two to three hours to navigate due to the blind curves and roadside dropoffs that fell straight into the ocean below. The road was well known for its stunning scenery. The average speed was only about fifteen miles per hour, and there were scenic overlooks but very few safe places to park.

Alex went down to the front desk of the hotel, keeping his cell phone on and pressed against his ear just in case he heard something new. He returned a few minutes later with brochures for Hana. What interested Alex the most was the confirmation that there was indeed a small airport used by private planes and general aviation. Was Carver going to kill her immediately or did he have plans to take her off the island?

Alex muted his cell phone and filled Delaney in on what he had overheard and learned about the area. Delaney in turn issued orders to the various agents to follow up on the leads, sending one to the computer to find out where Carver's uncle's house was in Hana, one to the local judge to obtain a search warrant and another to notify local law enforcement in Hana and in Kahului. A surge of hope swelled in Alex's chest. Chelsea's smart thinking had just given them an excellent advantage.

The marshal gave Alex a pat on the back. "Don't worry, Mr. Sullivan. We'll find her now. She's got a good head on her shoulders. Keep listening to see if she tells you what kind of vehicle they're in or any other hints that could help us out."

"I'm going with you to Hana," he said forcefully in his most severe lawyer tone, leaving absolutely no room for debate.

"I wouldn't advise that, Mr. Sullivan. You're an attorney, not law enforcement. You haven't had the proper training. Leave her rescue to the professionals. We'll be leaving shortly and can coordinate our efforts with the local authorities."

Alex barely held on to his temper. "By the time you're finished coordinating everything, Chelsea could be dead! I'm going to Hana and I'm going right now. Are you with me or not?"

Delaney seemed to consider Alex's words, apparently realizing from the timbre of the lawyer's voice that Alex would never yield unless Delaney literally cuffed him to the furniture to keep him away from their investigation. "All right. As long as she has a signal on that cell phone, we can track her with the phone's GPS. Let's hit the road."

"Good." Alex left the room and headed downstairs to wait for their car, still pressing the cell phone to his ear in the hope of getting something else valuable from Chelsea's conversation. So far, they hadn't said anything new, but Alex was happy just to have a lifeline into Chelsea's situation. It was a tenuous connection at best, but he would take anything at this point.

"Hold on, Chelsea," he whispered as he got in the car. "Hold on."

EIGHTEEN

The restaurant parking lot was filled with cars from the lunch crowd as Chelsea's abductor pulled around the back of the building and parked. He got out of the car and came around to Chelsea's side to pull her out. Chelsea didn't see much point in struggling since the man was twice her size and still had his gun strapped to his chest.

He pushed her toward the wall and she stumbled but somehow managed to keep from falling. She was still gripping her duffel bag, but the man grabbed it away from her and threw it on the ground. It landed against the wall.

"You won't be needing that anymore." The man's voice was a sneer. "In fact, you won't be needing much of anything."

Before Chelsea could even think of a response, a dark green limo pulled up next to them. The windows were tinted so it was impossible to see inside, but the back door opened before the vehicle had even come to a complete stop.

Justin Carver jumped out, dressed in a beige linen suit with a navy silk shirt and shiny leather dress shoes.

He was wearing his hair a little longer since the murder and he was thinner, but when he pulled off his sunglasses, his cold, dark eyes were exactly as she remembered them. The fake police officer from the hotel, who had given his name as Shepard, was also with him, and a third man who appeared to be the driver. Carver approached Chelsea and gave her a wicked smile, his breath polluting her face.

"Remember me?"

Chelsea tried to back up, but she was already against the outside wall of the restaurant, and there was really no place for her to go. She turned her head, refusing to look at him.

"Of course I remember you. You're the one I saw murder your own father in cold blood."

Carver's hand flew back as if to strike her, but then he stopped, his smile turning into a frown. "You've led me on quite a chase, Cecilia. But don't worry. I'll make sure your vacation in Maui ends with a bang." He slid his hand along her cheek, tracing over the scar he'd given her, and she shuddered in revulsion. "I hope you were anticipating this moment as much as I was. I've been searching for you all across the United States. Ever since my father died, I've been thinking of your face, and what I was going to do to you when our paths finally crossed again." He leaned in closely. "I've been looking forward to this day for a long, long time."

Chelsea pulled back, sickened by his words. "The police are onto you, Carver. I've told them all about how you murdered your father, and you're not going to get away with it. They'll track you down. They're looking for you as we speak. If you hurt me, too, you'll end up in prison even sooner, and not even your huge team of lawyers will be able to get you out." Her bluff sounded weak even to her ears, and he laughed at her threats.

Carver's tone was low and sinister when he spoke. "Of all of the lives in danger right now, Cecilia Rigo, maybe the one you should focus on is your own."

He nodded to the driver of the limo who was holding a dull red backpack. The driver tossed the backpack to the man who had abducted her, and he unzipped it and looked inside. Chelsea could just make out several bundles of cash and noted the man's satisfied smile.

She turned her attention back to Carver, who had stepped back and was talking to the driver again. Her eyes darted around nervously, but there was really no-where for her to go to escape. If she tried to run at this point they would probably just shoot her right here in the parking lot. Before she could even consider her next move, or decide if she even had one, Shepard grabbed her by the upper arm and pulled her toward the back of the limo. He opened the trunk and pulled out a roll of duct tape, which he used to secure her wrists behind her back. Then he roughly turned her around and put a strip across her mouth. With a shove he pushed her into the trunk and slammed the lid. She heard him settle in his seat in the limo as the driver started the engine.

Chelsea was trembling with fear and could feel her eyes tearing up as she shook in the darkness. Her arms hurt from the awkward angle and she had scraped her cheek against something sharp in the trunk. She couldn't waste time crying, however. She needed to think. She needed to pray. If she couldn't figure a way out of this, Carver would win, and her life would be over. She struggled to keep the tears at bay and also to keep breathing out of her nose since the tape stopped her from breathing through her mouth. She took several deep breaths as she felt the car turn and leave the parking lot.

Dear God. I know Your word promises You will never leave me or forsake me. Please help me stay calm and figure a way out of this.

Although the position of her hands made exploring difficult, she rolled slightly and tried to feel if there was anything else in the trunk with her. She could feel the tape biting into her wrists, but she pulled against her bindings anyway, knowing that finding a way out of the trunk was her only hope of survival.

After a few minutes she decided there didn't seem to be much in the trunk except for her. She did find a box that felt like a small cooler. It had textured sides and appeared to be the right size and shape to carry six cans of soda and maybe a sandwich or two. She kept scooting her body around until she bumped up against what seemed to be a small suitcase. Her fingers traced the outline of the case and felt for the zipper to pull to open it. Her arms ached with the awkward movements she was making, but desperation made her ignore the pain.

The driver took one of the curves a little too fast and her body rolled away from the suitcase and slammed into the back of the trunk like a sack of potatoes. A sob welled up within her and she started to pray once again, trying as best she could to block out the pain.

"It's right up here," Delaney said as he steered into the restaurant parking lot. They were in Alex's new rental car, but Delaney was driving so Alex could keep his ear pressed against his cell phone. He hadn't heard anything new in quite a while, but he didn't want to give up in case she was still close to the phone. Both men scanned the cars they passed as they drove, looking for any sign of Chelsea or anything else that might give them a clue as to her whereabouts.

Finally, Delaney pulled the car to the side of the lot outside a restaurant and parked. Alex reached for the door handle, but Delaney's voice stopped him.

"Stay in the car. We're waiting for backup."

Alex turned on him, his eyes burning fire. "We're wasting time. I haven't heard anything new on her phone for over fifteen minutes. I don't even think she's got it anymore. Carver is long gone from here and probably already on the road to Hana."

"You may be right," Delaney acknowledged, "but we're going to do this by the book. I'm not going to have a civilian messing up my crime scene if there turns out to be more here than we expect. Help will be here in ten minutes or less. According to the boys tracking her, she's still in the area, or at least her phone is."

"That's too long to wait," Alex growled, and reached again for the door handle. He had let Chelsea down at the hotel. He wasn't going to do it again now that they had such a solid lead.

"Step outside this car, Mr. Sullivan, and that will be the end of your involvement in this investigation," Delaney threatened, his voice like steel. "I told you, we're doing this by the book. I don't want anyone put in danger unnecessarily."

Alex sat back, frustration clearly written across his face, but there was nothing he could do but wait. A few

minutes later, two other U.S. marshal cars pulled into
the lot and Delaney again ordered Alex to stay in the
vehicle while the men swept the restaurant. They found
no signs of Chelsea and no witnesses that had seen anyone matching her description. The men returned to the
parking lot and spread out, walking slowly, scanning
the ground and the inside of the patrons' cars, hoping
to find some sign of Chelsea or her phone.

A patch of blue behind some weeds caught the eye of
one of the men and a few seconds later he was waving
the bag above his head and shouting to the other officers. Delaney joined them and the two of them sorted
through the contents. A few minutes later he left the
officer to bag the evidence and walked over to Alex
who was still watching the scene unfold from the car.

"We found her phone, but there's still no sign of
Chelsea. There are two sets of car tracks near where
the bag was left, so we're thinking they've switched
vehicles." He rubbed his face in a thoughtful gesture.
"Hopefully, the fact that the phone was still on and had
been discarded so carelessly means that Carver's men
didn't discover Chelsea's quick thinking and won't alter
their plans of taking her to Hana."

Delaney's words fueled Alex's impatience. "Let's go
then. Every second we waste could mean her life." One
way or another, Alex was done waiting for Delaney,
and the older agent must have sensed this. He nodded
and jumped back into the car, driving them out toward
the road to Hana.

Chelsea felt the car start curving and realized that
they had left the small town of Paia and were probably already past Hookipa Beach Park. From what she

remembered from the maps she'd seen, the rest of the drive for at least an hour would be winding curves and turns. Her stomach was already tightened in fear, and the lurching of the car wasn't helping, and they had only just begun the road to Hana. She willed herself to calm down and concentrate on her escape.

Dear God. Please help me. I'm so scared, but I know You are always with me. Help me stay focused and get out of this somehow.

She opened her eyes slowly and stared out into the blackness. It suddenly occurred to her that it wasn't completely dark, and she focused for a moment on her surroundings. There was a glow coming from the trunk latch. She scooted around until she get a good view and for the first time realized that the latch had a glow-in-the-dark handle so someone could use it to get out if they accidently got stuck in the trunk. That would be great—if she could actually get free of her bindings. She pulled against the tape that bound her wrists but it held fast. She knew from past experience that duct tape was almost impossible to tear. The first order of business had to be to find a way to cut that tape.

The light from the latch wasn't bright enough to help her to see what else might be in the trunk so she scooted around and tried to feel the shapes again. She rolled until she was pressed up against the small cooler—then pulled against it until she managed to tip it over.

"Oh!" She gasped as the lid came off and cold water and ice sloshed against her back. Two glass bottles clinked together and rolled around her as she tried to move away from the icy water. Suddenly an idea formed. Could she break one of the bottles and use the glass to cut the tape that held her wrists? At first she thought it was a good idea, but the more she pondered it, the more she decided it would be really hard to cut the tape without also cutting her wrists. She pushed the idea to the back of her mind but resolved to try it if she couldn't figure out anything else.

She awkwardly scooted over to the suitcase and fumbled with the zipper again until she had it opened. Maybe there was something in there that would help her. She felt clothes and a pair of shoes, and then a small leather bag. She pulled it out and yanked against the zipper of the smaller bag, hoping that she would find a shaving kit inside.

Please God. Have there be something in here I can use to get out of here.

She felt inside and discovered several small bottles and an electric razor. Desperation welled within her and she again concentrated on staying calm and focused on the task facing her. She put her hands back in the bag. An open straight razor sliced into the tender pad of her finger and she grimaced and pulled back. The car took a curve too fast and she was slung across the trunk again. She lay there for a minute, trying to regroup and quell the panic. Did she really have a chance of getting out of this mess?

NINETEEN

If Delaney didn't start driving faster, Alex was going to go insane. He watched the older man carefully, his mounting frustration nearly overwhelming him.

"Do you think you could go a little faster?" He tried to keep the irritation out of his voice, but the bitterness seeped through.

Alex's sarcasm wasn't wasted on Delaney. "I know you're worried about her, Mr. Sullivan, but flying over the ledge because I took a turn too fast doesn't seem like the best way to help her." He brushed an itch on his nose. "Might I also remind you that we still don't know what kind of car they are in, or precisely where their destination is? Racing down the road isn't going to solve anything."

"Neither will going five miles per hour."

"I can always pull over and let you walk back to your hotel."

Alex glared at him. "Just tell me they got the road-block set up."

Delaney nodded. "Yes, that's a go."

Alex gritted his teeth. At least one thing was going right. If the roadblock wasn't successful, though, he knew they were running out of options.

* * *

Chelsea pulled the small bag all the way out of the larger suitcase and stilled, her arms aching so badly that her fingers were going numb. She felt blindly inside the bag, trying to avoid the straight razor but knowing she could very well slice her finger a second time if she wasn't careful. She felt and identified nail clippers. Was there nothing in here to help her without also endangering her? She didn't think she could get the razor at the right angle to actually cut through the tape, but it was better than nothing. Was there anything else in there? She found ChapStick and a small square box of dental floss, and then her fingers felt the smooth metal of a small pair of scissors. Her heart soared. Could she somehow cut the tape?

A bump in the road caused the scissors to slip from her fingers and she frantically felt around the trunk carpet, hoping to locate them again. Her efforts were rewarded and she tried to maneuver the scissors in such a way that she could cut the binding off of her wrists. The tape had worked its way down and was now in a tight wad around her wrists. She braced her legs, hoping to keep herself from rolling as she concentrated on cutting through the tape, one small cut at a time. Suddenly she felt the car slow and then stop completely. Her heart beat frantically against her chest. Had she just run out of time?

She doubled her efforts on the tape. Finally she cut the last thread of it and pulled, freeing her arms. She took a moment to stretch out the soreness, then reached up and yanked the tape off her mouth with one quick pull. The pain was immediate, but so was the breath of air that filled her lungs. The car still hadn't moved. She stretched her muscles the best she could and rolled over to the latch. With a quick flick she opened the trunk and stumbled out onto the pavement. She couldn't see what was causing the problem, but the cars were backed up in both lanes and traffic had come to an absolute standstill. On the left was a sheer drop of about a hundred feet to jagged rocks below. On the right was a wall of rock that eventually gave way to vegetation that covered the side of the mountain. Cars were already piling up behind the limo, and there was no way for the driver to turn or to get around the traffic. Carver's car was completely stuck in the gridlock.

The situation surprised her but she rapidly took it all in and then ran as quickly as she could away from Carver and his minions.

She darted around the dark blue sedan that was behind the limo, then passed a red convertible, ignoring the stares of the drivers and passengers. She stumbled on some gravel and hit the ground hard, but the fear that gripped her drove her back to her feet again. She started to run past the next car in the line as she brushed away the small stones that had stuck to her skin. She had only one thought in her mind—to get as far from Carver as possible.

When she was about fifty feet away, she dared a look behind her. Justin was out of the limo and swaggering in her direction with cocky sureness in every step. She saw him pat his side and noticed a bulge that had to be a pistol under his jacket. Running down the road made her an easy target, she realized. Her only chance was to escape into the mountainside and hope she could lose him in the rainforest. With a burst of determination, she darted into the woods.

* * *

Delaney was able to get Alex within about a mile of the roadblock, but the cars had backed up considerably already and there was simply no way to turn around or to get past the narrow bridges to continue around the mountain. Impatient drivers honked their horns, but the quagmire would take hours to unravel.

The phone rang and Delaney had a brief, terse conversation before he snapped his phone shut and turned to his passenger. "Chelsea got away from Carver. It looks like she had been locked in the trunk of Carver's limo, then somehow she got away from him at the roadblock and ran up into the woods by the road. Apparently some of the drivers in the other cars saw her escape and called it in to the police. They've got the limo driver in custody and another man that was in the vehicle, but Carver is nowhere to be seen. A few of the motorists said a man fitting his description followed Chelsea up the mountainside into the jungle. They said she's heading in our direction."

Alex reached for the door handle but Delaney grabbed his arm before he could open the door. "Do we have to go through this again? It's obvious you care about her, but you've got to let the police handle this. You'd only get in the way up there. Stay in the vehicle."

Alex had had enough of watching. It was time to act. Somewhere on the side of the mountain, Chelsea was running for her life. He couldn't leave her to face Justin Carver alone. He knew that if Carver was alone with Chelsea for long, she wouldn't survive the encounter. He also knew the odds of finding her were probably slim. There were acres and acres of land where she could be hiding and he was at least a mile from where she had gone off into the jungle. He said a silent prayer as he considered his next move. He wasn't much of an outdoors man and he knew he could get lost on the mountainside, but he had to try. He couldn't live with himself if he didn't do everything within his power to help her. With the decision made, he pulled his arm away from Delaney's grasp.

"I have to help her."

"Let law enforcement handle it."

"No." Alex got out of the car and Delaney quickly followed him and grabbed his arm again.

"Sullivan, I can't let you go up there. You have to let the professionals take it from here. They've called in a K-9 unit and a helicopter. If you go up there you're just going to get in the way. You could get hurt or lost, and then they'll have to spend time helping you instead of helping Chelsea."

"By the time they get here, Chelsea could be dead!" Alex stated emphatically in a tone that was low and threatening. "There's a murderer on the loose and he's chasing her down. You know just as well as I do what Carver is capable of doing to her if he finds her before the police do. I don't have time to argue with you. I'm going up that mountain." His eyes blazed with ferociousness but Delaney didn't back down.

"You're interfering in an official investigation. If you keep going up that hill, you'll be headed straight for a jail cell right next to Carver's. You'll lose your freedom first and then your license to practice law."

Alex gritted his teeth and shook his head. "I'll lose more than that if I don't go." He paused and looked the agent straight in the eye. "You do what you have to do, Delaney. You can't legally stop me from walking away from this car and into the woods. I'm not in your custody, and I'm going after Chelsea."

"I won't be able to protect you if you go against Carver on your own. You know that, don't you? You could get caught in the crossfire and your next stop could be the county morgue."

"Thanks for the warning, but I'm going." He started running toward the foliage, half expecting Delaney to try to stop him as he started climbing. He dared a look over his shoulder. Delaney was on the phone glaring at him, but had returned to his car. Alex turned back to the forest in front of him, praying that he could find Chelsea before it was too late.

TWENTY

Someone was chasing her. She heard the sounds of the leaves crunching behind her but was too scared to turn and face her pursuer. Whoever it was, he was relentless, which made her chill with fear. It had to be Carver. No one else would keep up this chase through the thick Hawaiian forest. How long had she been running away from the limo? Thirty minutes? An hour? Two? Plant vegetation was thick and made her progress slow, but she knew it slowed down whoever was chasing her, as well, and she was grateful for the cover it gave her.

A new sound emerged and she stopped for a moment to listen. Her breath came in gasps and her muscles ached and trembled. She knew she couldn't keep going much longer. She tried to steady her breathing and to concentrate on the sounds around her. She could just make out the sound of a waterfall, and headed that direction with all of her strength. She suddenly broke through a stand of large leafy plants and found herself in a clearing, looking out toward one of the most beautiful sights she had ever seen. A large waterfall fell nearly forty feet into a wide pool and was framed with blooming tropical foliage. A fine mist rose from the water and kissed all the nearby plants with moisture. Boulders lined the area and added the finishing touches to the picturesque setting. The view alone made her ache to rest and cool off in the water. She moaned and tamped down those thoughts as she continued her ascent over the rocks. Right now, survival was the only thought that mattered.

"That's far enough, don't you think?" The sneer in Carver's voice sent chills down Chelsea's spine. She froze, a sense of desperation washing over her as she slowly turned to face him.

Carver was standing only a few yards behind her with a bitter scowl on his face. He was apparently not used to climbing mountains, and it showed in the way he carried himself. He was tired and flushed, and sweat glistened on his forehead, but he was also pointing a 9 mm pistol right at her chest.

She sat back wearily on one of the boulders, her muscles trembling with exhaustion. She didn't have a lot of fight left in her, and was unable to do a single thing to stop Carver as he approached. At this point, she wasn't even sure if she could stand up again without toppling over. The gun in his hand made resistance futile anyway. She had no way to defend herself against the weapon and was at the mercy of the madman in front of her.

In just a few moments he towered above her and smiled, his mouth curved into a hideous show of domination. "Did you really think I'd let you live?" His voice was icy and Chelsea felt a slash of fear strike her heart. "Did you think I wouldn't silence you forever?"

"They'll find you," she spat out defiantly. "If you

kill me, they'll hunt you down like the animal you are—"

The slap silenced her and drew blood from the corner of her mouth. When he spoke, his voice was low and threatening. "Your problem is you don't know when to keep your mouth shut," he said severely. He studied his surroundings and smiled again as an idea apparently started to take shape. "Let's continue this little walk together, shall we?" With a cruel grip he grasped her hair and yanked her to her feet. She cried out in pain but managed to stand.

"We're headed up. Do you hear me? Start moving across these rocks and up that hill." He motioned at some trees ahead of her and pushed her toward them, releasing her in the process. She took a moment to gather herself and then gingerly stepped over the boulders, looking for footholds as she went. Fear gave her a second wind of energy, but she knew it wouldn't last long; her limbs were still trembling with effort.

"You won't get away with this," Chelsea rasped as she climbed. "They know you abducted me. They know you were out here following me." She paused and tried to steady her breathing. "The man you paid to grab me at the dock attacked a U.S. Marshal. The feds will be at every airport, every harbor and at every other conceivable way off this island looking for you so they can arrest you and haul you off to jail. You're stuck, Carver. Even if you kill me, you'll never get off Maui a free man."

"They'll have to have proof before they arrest me, Cecilia, and if you haven't noticed yet, I'm very talented at getting out of sticky situations. No one can prove that I was the one who abducted you—or even that I knew you were in the trunk of my car before you came popping out. All the witnesses will be able to say for sure is that once you ran off, I came out here after you. For all they'll know, I followed you to try to help you, but was unable to keep you from falling. They'll probably even call me a hero. Law enforcement does not attract the best and brightest, and I have the best attorneys money can buy at my beck and call."

He stopped for a moment and wiped a handkerchief across his brow, a sneer on his face. "I'll be enjoying the surf and ordering piña coladas in no time at all." He looked at her directly and their eyes locked. "Chelsea Rogers, huh? That was the best name you could come up with? Don't you miss the name you were born with?"

She was so focused on watching him, waiting to see what he was going to do, that the rock that came flying toward them startled her as much as it did him. The rock hit Carver square in the right forearm and the pistol slipped from his grip and clattered down the rocks below them. Surprise lit his features, especially once he realized that the rock had come from behind him rather than from Chelsea's hand. He turned, holding his arm, and was hit with a second stone, this one on the right shoulder.

"Run, Chelsea!" Alex's voice yelled up to her, a third rock in his hand.

The shock of seeing Alex throwing rocks at Carver had left her frozen, but his voice spurred her into action and she turned and frantically clawed at the hill, climbing as fast as she could to get away from the madman below her.

* * *

Alex was still a good forty feet away from Carver and Chelsea, but thankfully his aim was good enough to knock the gun from the madman's hand. For the first time in years he appreciated his gift of pitching a fastball. Stones weren't exactly the same size and weight as the baseballs he'd thrown in the minor league, but they were close enough to slow Carver down and give Chelsea a lead as he chased her up the mountainside.

"The next time I'm aiming for your head!" Alex yelled at Carver. He let the third rock fly, but Carver ducked at just the right moment and it went bouncing harmlessly off of a tree behind his intended target. Alex quickly studied the ground around his feet, looking for another rock that was about the right size for him to throw. At this point he would be happy if he could just keep Carver from getting to Chelsea or his gun. Seeing only rocks that were too large to heave at his opponent, he started up the sharp incline, hoping to reach Carver and intercept him before he could reach Chelsea.

Carver paused a moment as if weighing his choices, then started up after Chelsea. He apparently realized he would have little chance to retrieve the gun before Alex was upon him, so his only chance was to grab Chelsea and use her as a hostage. He chased after her, his left arm still cradling the one that had been hit by the rocks.

Chelsea climbed as fast as she could and reached the plateau above the waterfall, her chest heaving. She was exhausted and knew her legs wouldn't carry her much longer. She was not used to such strenuous mountain climbing and her muscles trembled with exertion. She took another step and her left leg collapsed under her. She was finished. Her body knew it, even though her mind refused to give up.

She pulled herself to a sitting position and studied her surroundings. She was at the edge of the river that led to the waterfall and it rushed by her on its way to the rocks below. The water didn't look that deep and the current wasn't very fast, but with her energy spent, she didn't know if she could fight the current to keep from getting swept over the edge if she went into the water. One look behind her made her options disappear. Carver was only about ten feet behind and his eyes shone with a hatred she feared more than the waterfall. With a grunt of determination she threw herself into the water, keeping a wary eye on the brutal man behind her. Carver was still standing on the bank, watching her with an indecisive look on his face.

Chelsea discovered the water was only about five feet deep, and the stream only looked about thirty feet wide, but even so, in her exhausted state, she was having difficulty making it across. The current pushed at her mercilessly. She knew Carver was probably thinking that with any luck at all, the stream would do what he had planned to do himself—throw her over the waterfall.

The next rock came as unexpectedly as the first and hit Carver square in the back. As the criminal bent in pain, a second stone hit him in the leg and he lost his balance and fell into the water.

* * *

Alex was a mere thirty feet behind him this time and experience told him that the rocks had hit hard enough to crack bones.

Carver grasped in vain at the slick rocks around him. But his injuries and the current where he'd fallen in kept him floundering in the water until the water swept him away and out over the waterfall. His scream echoed off of the canyon walls as he was carried over the ledge.

Alex closed the distance as fast as he could between himself and the water's edge, scanning for Chelsea. At first he didn't see her, but then he caught sight of her dark brown hair floating in the water near an outcropping of rocks. She seemed dangerously close to following the same fate as Carver.

She wasn't moving! Was she even alive? A new wave of fear swept over him and he said a silent prayer as he rushed into the water, swimming in fast, frantic strokes until he reached her and pulled her close. She had somehow managed to grab some vegetation that was stuck between two rocks and had wrapped her arm around it. That narrow piece of weed was the only thing that had kept her from being swept over the falls. He gently disentangled her and swam the remaining few feet to the other side of the stream, dragging her exhausted body with him.

"Chelsea?" His voice was heavily laden with concern as he carried her up the bank and settled her on the ground. He ran his hands over her arms and legs, searching for broken bones or other injuries. "Are you okay?"

She gave him a tired smile. "I'm okay. I'm just worn

out." She reached up and touched his face gingerly. "What about you? I know that man at the hotel hurt you. Are you okay?"

"I'm fine," Alex reassured her. "A few bumps and bruises, that's all."

Her hand was trembling as she let it fall away. "How did you find me?"

Alex grabbed her hand and squeezed. "I've been working with the marshals. Turning on your cell phone and calling me was brilliant. They tracked you as far as the restaurant, then set up the roadblock. The other drivers from the roadblock reported that you'd gotten out of the trunk and run off out here. I had no idea if I could find you or not once you took to the woods, but I had to try." He gave her a small kiss on her forehead. "God led me right to you."

"I didn't want to call you because I didn't want to get you involved again, but I didn't know what else to do. I knew 9-1-1 wouldn't help."

Alex squeezed her hand again. "You did exactly the right thing. I was going crazy before you called. We knew what had happened at the dock and I couldn't figure out how to help you."

"Is Carver dead?"

Alex nodded. "He went over the waterfall."

She closed her eyes, as if gathering her strength, then opened them again and gazed at the man in front of her. "Thank you. You saved my life. Again."

Alex couldn't return the smile. He felt too stricken. "I could have lost you forever," he said softly, the impact of his words sending a coldness throughout his body. If he'd found them even a few minutes later, Carver would have succeeded in killing her. He knew

God had directed his path. He also knew that he never would have found her without God's intervention. He said a silent prayer of thanksgiving and pulled her close again, resting her head against his chest. "I love you, Chelsea. I've been so blind. Please forgive me."

"There's nothing to forgive." She turned her head and leaned back so that she could see his eyes. "I'm the one who was guarding so many secrets. I should have trusted you sooner..."

He silenced her with a kiss, gentle and sweet. "I love you so much." His lips moved to her cheeks and to her eyelids, then to her neck. "I love you, Chelsea," he said again, his voice raspy with emotion. "I could have lost you. I don't know what I would have done if I'd been too late." He took a deep breath and held her closely. "Come back to Tallahassee with me. Please? Say you'll come back and we'll give this a chance."

She didn't answer right away. Alex read her indecision instantly and gently caressed her cheek with his hand. "Before you answer, you should know that a few things have changed. If we're going to give this a go, our lives need to be built on something solid. From now on, faith and family come first." He gave her another soft kiss on her lips. "I'm not perfect, I know that, and I'm a work in progress, but maybe you can help me. What do you think?"

She sighed, a peaceful expression on her face. She looked into his eyes and he saw such love and devotion that it sent a wave of warmth through him.

"Yes, I'll come back to Tallahassee. I love you, too, Alex Sullivan."

Alex let out his breath, unaware that he had even been holding it. He gently rubbed his thumb over her bottom lip, then kissed her again where his thumb had touched. It was a sweet kiss, one filled with promise.

"God has truly blessed me, Chelsea Rogers. He led me right to you, and just in time."

"He's blessed me, too," she said softly, then laughed and squeezed his hand. "You must have been a pretty good pitcher back when you were playing ball."

Alex shrugged. "My fastball was clocked at over ninety miles per hour a couple of times. I was worried about my accuracy, but everything worked out for the best." He locked eyes with her. "Did he hurt you?"

"Not really," Chelsea said softly, "but I'll admit I was terrified. I didn't think I'd ever get out of that trunk alive." She went through the story of her capture and how she had escaped, hitting the highlights.

Alex studied her hands. The blood had been washed away but he saw the cuts and the bruises left from her struggles. That she had to go through such an experience made him seethe with anger. At least it was over now that Carver was dead. He took a breath and told her about the team of marshals that had descended upon Maui to find her and about all of their efforts since she had disappeared from the hotel. "The local police even stepped up to the plate, Chelsea. This whole area is probably going to be crawling with law enforcement in an hour or so."

She gave him a tired smile. "You know, it's okay if you want to call me Cecilia."

Alex stared at her a moment, then smiled. "I love you, Cecilia Eliana Rigo." He gave her a tender kiss.

They heard a shout from below. Alex gave Cecilia a squeeze and left her sitting on the bank to walk over to the ledge so he could see below the waterfall. Carver's body had smashed into the rocks and his lifeless form lay prone where it had fallen. Delaney was standing near Carver and looking for signs of life.

Alex called down to him and waved once he had the man's attention. Delaney waved back and spoke into a walkie-talkie. A few minutes later law-enforcement officers swarmed the area and helped to get everyone down the mountain.

It was finally over. Chelsea Rogers was free.

EPILOGUE

Six months later

Cecilia squeezed Alex's hand and sighed content-
edly. She watched as Alex accepted congratulations
from some friends that he knew through his church
and she smiled and greeted them as Alex made the
introductions.

They had just finished dessert at the dinner party on
Miss Abigail's veranda, and afterward stood and announced their engagement. The excitement of the day
still made her feel as if she was floating. Could a person die of happiness? A few months ago she had been
running for her life, afraid that if she had a future, it
would only be filled with loneliness—never letting
anyone close and always looking over her shoulder.
She never could have imagined that she would actually be here today, engaged to be married to the most
wonderful man in the world.

"Isn't this a beautiful day for a garden party?" Miss
Abigail cooed as she adjusted her hat. "The clouds
couldn't be more perfect if you had painted them in
the sky yourself."

She leaned in and gave Cecilia a kiss, then gave Alex a hug, as well. "Of course, my azaleas are done blooming, but the hydrangeas are just beginning their show and the roses are magnificent."

"You are absolutely right," Cecilia agreed, "and you did a great job with arranging the photo displays. You should have been a professional decorator." Several easels had been placed along the garden path, each holding a framed photograph that Cecilia had taken during their trip to Maui, culminating in an enlargement of a photo of Alex and Cecilia that had been taken on the beach in Maui only a few days after Alex had saved Cecilia's life at the river.

"There's still time," Miss Abigail declared with a twinkle in her eye. She squeezed Cecilia's hand, then gracefully fluttered among her guests, always the consummate hostess.

Cecilia knew she owed a lot to Miss Abigail. In fact, if Miss Abigail hadn't gotten Alex to come along on their Hawaiian trip, she'd probably be dead right now, and she definitely wouldn't be engaged. Not only had Alex saved Cecilia's life in Hawaii, but the elderly lady had also gotten Alex to take a closer look at his life and to reassess his priorities. Gone was the seventy-hour-a-week work schedule.

She leaned up and gave her fiancé a kiss on the cheek. He responded by hugging her close. She hoped that as their future together unfolded, she could help Alex slow down and learn to enjoy life and live well, and that he would continue to show her that trust could be a blessing.

Her eyes turned to Dominic, the youngest Sullivan son, who was also in attendance, and to Dominic's wife, Jessica, who was standing by his side. Dressed in a dark suit and sunglasses, Dominic was the epitome of a hard-hitting law-enforcement agent with broad shoulders and a tough, impenetrable appearance. Although she'd heard that he had always been the prankster of the three brothers as they were growing up, he apparently took his job very seriously and had garnered an excellent reputation at the U.S. Marshal's office. His help with her case had uncovered the fact that she had been recognized at the airport by Carver's henchman— the one she had come to think of as the Braves fan— something that she and Alex had wondered about. He had also discovered how Carver's man had been following and tracking Alex in Hawaii—by using computer software to track Alex's cell phone.

Because of Dominic and his team's efforts, Carver's crimes had been fully exposed and several arrests had already been made in both the embezzlement and the money laundering schemes. Carver Enterprises was now in receivership until the books could get straightened out and the board could appoint a temporary CEO in Carver's stead to point the company in a new direction. All in all, Chelsea knew that his professional handling of the case had gone a long way toward improving her views of law enforcement.

Her eyes surveyed the rest of the crowd that had gathered for the dinner party and she squeezed Alex's hand. "So, when does Ryan leave?" she asked, knowing that Alex and Ryan had already been making plans for his brother's upcoming departure. His unit had just been activated, and Ryan would soon be on a transport to the Middle East for his third tour in the Army JAG corps.

"On the sixteenth," Alex answered. "It's going to be here before we know it. I sure am going to miss him."

Cecilia knew it was going to be hard on Alex to have his brother gone from his life and their law firm once again. The two men were very close, especially since they had worked together for so long. They had another associate at the firm who could help cover the cases, but Cecilia knew Alex wouldn't feel completely at ease again until his brother was home safely from his tour of duty.

Apparently, Ryan was also a confirmed bachelor, and she wondered for a moment what kind of woman it would take to finally get him to the altar. Would Ryan be able to find happiness, the way she and Alex had found, with a bride of his own? She laughed to herself and considered the possibilities. With God, anything was possible.

* * * * *

Dear Reader,

One of Chelsea's best qualities is that she tried to help Miss Abigail, even though her life was in jeopardy. Selflessness is a rare quality these days, but God calls on us to love others around us, even if it isn't convenient. In fact, I believe that it is often during the difficult times that God uses us the most.

My prayer for you, dear reader, is that you find a way to get involved in helping others. Maybe you can become a foster parent, or even an adoptive parent of a needy child. Maybe you can take meals to those dealing with sickness or loss. The choices are infinite, and with God leading your path, you can quickly become an instrument of love and compassion right in your own community. It may not be convenient. It probably won't be easy, and there will probably be obstacles that appear at every turn. Yet when we help others and truly give of ourselves, we will be rewarded in ways that we never expect.

May God bless you as you discover the path that God has for you as you search for His will in your life. Remember John 15:13: Greater love has no one than this, that one lay down his life for his friends. NIV.

Kathleen Tailer

Questions for Discussion

1. In the beginning, Chelsea tries to handle her problems by herself without leaning on God. Have you ever tried to do that in your own life? What was the result?

2. After Chelsea witnesses the murder of Roderick Carver, she fails to go to the police to report the crime. Was this the right decision? Why or why not?

3. Alex is concerned about Chelsea's motives, but he never really comes right out and asks her if she is trying to cheat Miss Abigail. Should he have been more direct? Would it have made a difference?

4. Chelsea didn't trust Alex with her secrets because of her past. Have you ever trusted someone that let you down?

5. Do you trust God? Why or why not?

6. After the murder Chelsea has to leave Chicago, but she decides to relocate somewhere where she can help someone else and make something good come out of a bad situation. Have you ever turned a bad situation into something that helped others?

7. See Genesis 50:20. How is this story in the Bible similar to Chelsea's situation?

8. Alex made his job his number-one priority. Do you have anything in your life that has pushed God out of your life?

9. What does God's Word say should come first?

10. What are Alex's best qualities? How does he use them in this story?

11. What are Chelsea's best traits? Do they help her in Hawaii? Why or why not?

12. What are Chelsea's flaws? Do you share any of them? If so, what have you done to try to overcome them?

13. After Alex and Chelsea returned to Tallahassee, what did they do to improve their relationship?

14. What does this verse mean to you? "Trust in the Lord with all your heart, and lean not on your own understanding; in all your ways acknowledge Him, and He shall direct your paths." Proverbs 3:5-6 NKJV. What do you think it means to Chelsea and Alex?

15. Out of all of the characters in the book, which one needed God the most?

COMING NEXT MONTH FROM
Love Inspired® Suspense

Available December 2, 2014

HER CHRISTMAS GUARDIAN
Mission: Rescue • by Shirlee McCoy

Scout Cramer's young daughter is kidnapped while Scout is on the run from her troubled past. Can hostage rescue expert Boone Anderson risk his life—and his heart—to bring them together again?

THE YULETIDE RESCUE
Alaskan Search and Rescue • by Margaret Daley

A plane crash leaves Dr. Aubrey Mathison stranded in the Alaskan wilderness during the Christmas season. Search and Rescue leader David Stone arrives just in time, but together they'll discover there are more dangers lurking on the snowy horizon.

COLD CASE JUSTICE • by Sharon Dunn

Rochelle Miller thinks she's left her past behind as a witness to murder, until the criminal reappears. This time when she runs, she'll have handsome paramedic Matthew Stewart to keep her son safe...and the killer at bay.

NAVY SEAL NOEL
Men of Valor • by Liz Johnson

Abducted by a drug cartel, Jessalynn McCoy must rely on her former best friend—navy SEAL Will Gumble—to get her home in time for Christmas. But can she bring herself to trust the man who left her behind years ago?

SILVER LAKE SECRETS • by Alison Stone

After her life is put on the line, Nicole Braun refuses to allow her little boy to get caught up in the danger. Too bad the only one she can trust to protect her, police chief Brett Eggert, also has the power to break her heart.

TREACHEROUS INTENT • by Camy Tang

It's Liam O'Neill's job as a skip tracer to find private investigator Elisabeth Aday's missing client. When rival gangs come after them for information, they're thrown together in a race against the clock.

LISCNM1114

REQUEST YOUR FREE BOOKS!
2 FREE RIVETING INSPIRATIONAL NOVELS
PLUS 2 FREE MYSTERY GIFTS

YES! Please send me 2 FREE Love Inspired® Suspense novels and my 2 FREE mystery gifts (gifts are worth about $10). After receiving them, if I don't wish to receive any more books, I can return the shipping statement marked "cancel." If I don't cancel, I will receive 4 brand-new novels every month and be billed just $4.74 per book in the U.S. or $5.24 per book in Canada. That's a savings of at least 21% off the cover price. It's quite a bargain! Shipping and handling is just 50¢ per book in the U.S. and 75¢ per book in Canada.* I understand that accepting the 2 free books and gifts places me under no obligation to buy anything. I can always return a shipment and cancel at any time. Even if I never buy another book, the two free books and gifts are mine to keep forever.

123/323 IDN F5AC

Name	(PLEASE PRINT)	

Address		Apt. #

City	State/Prov.	Zip/Postal Code

Signature (if under 18, a parent or guardian must sign)

Mail to the Harlequin® Reader Service:
IN U.S.A.: P.O. Box 1867, Buffalo, NY 14240-1867
IN CANADA: P.O. Box 609, Fort Erie, Ontario L2A 5X3

Are you a current subscriber to Love Inspired Suspense books and want to receive the larger-print edition?
Call 1-800-873-8635 or visit www.ReaderService.com.

* Terms and prices subject to change without notice. Prices do not include applicable taxes. Sales tax applicable in N.Y. Canadian residents will be charged applicable taxes. Offer not valid in Quebec. This offer is limited to one order per household. Not valid for current subscribers to Love Inspired Suspense books. All orders subject to credit approval. Credit or debit balances in a customer's account(s) may be offset by any other outstanding balance owed by or to the customer. Please allow 4 to 6 weeks for delivery. Offer available while quantities last.

Your Privacy—The Harlequin® Reader Service is committed to protecting your privacy. Our Privacy Policy is available online at www.ReaderService.com or upon request from the Harlequin Reader Service.
We make a portion of our mailing list available to reputable third parties that offer products we believe may interest you. If you prefer that we not exchange your name with third parties, or if you wish to clarify or modify your communication preferences, please visit us at www.ReaderService.com/consumerschoice or write to us at Harlequin Reader Service Preference Service, P.O. Box 9062, Buffalo, NY 14269. Include your complete name and address.

"Robin," Ethan said, just before his face appeared in the church belfry's open trapdoor, "come on up. It's perfectly safe."

He reached down a gloved hand as she put a foot on the bottom rung of the wrought-iron ladder.

"How does this thing work?"

"It's very simple. There's a tall pole with a hook on one end. I used it to slide open the trap and then pull down the ladder. When I'm done, I'll use it to push the ladder back up and lift it over the locking mechanism, then slide the trap closed."

"I see."

"Oh, you haven't seen anything yet," he told her, grasping her hand and all but lifting her up the last few rungs to stand next to him on a narrow metal platform. In their bulky coats, they had to stand pressed shoulder to shoulder. "Take a look at this." He swung his arm wide, encompassing the town, the valley beyond and the snow-capped mountains surrounding it all.

"Wow."

"Exactly," he said. "There's a part of Psalms 98 that says, 'Let the rivers clap their hands, let the mountains sing together for joy…' Seeing the view like this, you can almost feel it, can't you? The rivers and mountains praising their Creator."

"I never thought of rivers and mountains praising God," she admitted.

"Scripture speaks many times of nature praising God and testifying to His wonders."

"I can see why," she said reverently.

"So can I," he told her, smiling down at her with those warm brown eyes.

Her breath caught in her throat. But surely she was reading too much into that look. That wasn't appreciation she saw in his gaze. That was just her loneliness seeking connection. Wasn't it? Though she had never felt this sudden, electrical link before, as if something vital and masculine in him reached out and touched something fundamental and feminine in her. She had to be mistaken.

He was a man of God, after all.

Even if she couldn't help thinking of him as just a man.

Will Robin and Ethan find love for Christmas,
or will her secrets stand in their way?
Find out in HER MONTANA CHRISTMAS
by Arlene James, available December 2014 wherever
Love Inspired® books and ebooks are sold.

"Just tell me what happened to my daughter."

"We don't know. You were alone when we found you."

"I need to go home." Scout jumped up, head spinning,
the room spinning. The knot in her stomach growing until
it was all she could feel. "Maybe she's there."

She knew it was unreasonable, knew it couldn't be
true, but she had to look, had to be sure.

"The police have already been to your house," Boone
said gently. "She's not there."

"She could be hiding. She doesn't like strangers." Her
voice trembled. Her body trembled, every fear she'd ever
had, every nightmare, suddenly real and happening and
completely outside her control.

"Scout." He touched her shoulder, his fingers warm
through thin cotton. She didn't want warmth, though. She
wanted her child.

"Please," she begged. "I have to go home. I have to see
for myself. I have to."

He eyed her for a moment, silent. Solemn. Something
in his eyes that looked like the grief she was feeling, the
horror she was living.

Finally, Boone nodded. "Okay. I'll take you."

Just like that. Simple and easy, as if the request didn't

go against logic. As if she weren't hooked to an IV, shaking from fear and sorrow and pain.

He grabbed a blanket from the foot of the bed and wrapped it around her shoulders then took out his phone and texted someone. She didn't ask who. She was too busy trying to keep the darkness from taking her again. Too busy trying to remember the last moment she'd seen Lucy. Had she been scared? Crying?

Three days.

That was what he had said.

Three days that Lucy had been missing and Scout had been lying in a hospital bed.

Please, God, let her be okay.

She was all Scout had. The only thing that really mattered to her. She had to be okay.

A tear slipped down her cheek. She didn't have the energy to wipe it away. Didn't have the strength to even open her eyes when Boone touched her cheek.

"It's going to be okay," he said quietly, and she wanted to believe him almost as much as she wanted to open her eyes and see her daughter.

"How can it be?"

"Because you ran into the right person the night your daughter was taken," he responded, and he sounded so confident, so certain of the outcome, she looked into his face, his eyes. Saw those things she'd seen before, but something else, too—faith, passion, belief.

Will Boone help Scout find her missing
daughter in time for Christmas?
Pick up HER CHRISTMAS GUARDIAN to find out!
Available December 2014
wherever Love Inspired® books and ebooks are sold.

Love Inspired®
SUSPENSE
RIVETING INSPIRATIONAL ROMANCE

THE YULETIDE RESCUE
by
MARGARET DALEY

MISTLETOE AND MURDER

When Dr. Bree Mathison's plane plummets into the Alaskan wilderness at Christmastime, she is torn between grief and panic. With the pilot—her dear friend—dead and wolves circling, she struggles to survive. Search and Rescue leader David Stone fights his way through the elements to save her. David suspects the plane crash might not have been an accident, spurring Bree's sense that she's being watched. But why is someone after her? Suddenly Bree finds herself caught in the middle of a whirlwind of secrets during the holiday season. With everyone she cares about most in peril, Bree and her promised protector must battle the Alaskan tundra and vengeful criminals to make it to the New Year.

ALASKAN
+ SEARCH RESCUE

Risking their lives to save the day

Available December 2014
wherever Love Inspired
books and ebooks are sold.

Find us on Facebook at
www.Facebook.com/LoveInspiredBooks

LIS44637

Love Inspired

An Amish Christmas Journey
by
Patricia Davids

Their Holiday Adventure

Toby Yoder promised to care for his orphaned little sister the rest of her life. After all, the tragedy that took their parents and left her injured was his fault. Now he must make a three-hundred-mile trip from the hospital to the Amish community where they'll settle down. But as they share a hired van with pretty Greta Barkman, an Amish woman with a similar harrowing past, Toby can't bear for the trip to end. Suddenly, there's joy, a rescued cat named Christmas and hope for their journey to continue together forever.

BRIDES OF *Amish Country*

Finding true love in the land of the Plain People

*Available December 2014
wherever Love Inspired books
and ebooks are sold.*

LI87927